Lin.

Every day
we really
live and love
is a Mysterious
Adventure.

Rose Gordy

MW01596431

THE LADIES BALTIMORE

Mothers and Daughters Alone and Together

Rose Gordy

ISBN 978-1456311308

Rosewords Books
www.Rosewords.com

Front cover watercolor painting by
Rose Gordy and Stephen Charles

To my sister Pat

who was with me when....

Table of Contents

PART I   Sister Eustacia – Slipping Away

PART II   Naomi - Holding On

PART III   Aiesha - Coming Together

PART I

SISTER EUSTACIA
Slipping Away

"What'll I do
When you are far away
And I am blue
What'll I do....
When I'm alone with only dreams of you
That won't come true, what'll I do."

(Irving Berlin 1923)

Chapter 1

A Father's Anger

"Careful. Careful, James," the young man warned his co-worker. The elderly nun named Sister Eustacia felt them slowly lift her wheelchair onto the gangplank of the luncheon cruise boat on the Baltimore Harbor. Was that her James? Her James from so long ago. Over six feet tall with dark curly hair and an engaging smile. Oh yes and mesmerizing blue-green eyes....

Four other nuns from the retirement wing of the Motherhouse had come along to help celebrate her ninety-fifth birthday. What stood out about Sister Eustacia at first glance was her updated short veil perched off-center on her head. Actually, it seemed to be an indication of her mental state which flowed in and out of lucidity with almost every other breath she took. She sat in her wheelchair surrounded by her fellow sisters and their aides at a table in the middle of the room, all of them waiting for the hot luncheon of grilled chicken, green beans and parsley potatoes to be served.

Out of the corner of her eye, Sister Eustacia noticed one of the "African American" girls, as she called them, from the group of high school students at several long tables to her right grin at her. She couldn't understand why this young woman wearing tight blue jeans with a wide silver belt and a blue shirt with a swooping neckline would make eye contact with her. Still Sister smiled back and then closed her eyes as she heard a familiar voice call out to her out of the blue....

"Mary, haven't you finished packing yet?"

"Yes, Mother, just about."

"Remember we're leaving at noon on the Maiden Voyage of the Ile de France. It'll dock in Le Havre and then we'll take a train to Paris where your Father has reserved a delightful suite of rooms for us in one of the best hotels in the city."

"Yes, Mother, Father told me all about it. It all sounds so absolutely wonderful!"

"Did he tell you we're traveling First Class all the way too?"

"Yes, he did, Mother. Oh what terrific fun we'll have and all to celebrate my sixteenth birthday! Father's outdone himself this time."

Sister Eustacia remembered every fine detail of those

days in the summer of '28 and her birthday celebration on August 24th! How excited she had been ahead of time thinking about this very special present from her parents - going on the first voyage of a new ship all the way across the Atlantic Ocean....

But today on this other boat for some reason she couldn't fathom, she wasn't sure how old she was or even what year it was, but that didn't concern her now because she was boarding the huge ocean liner with her parents. Her Father had just introduced her to James, the son of one of his business associates. Oh, he was so handsome with dark black curly hair and blue-green eyes so piercing she could hardly look directly at them for more than a few seconds at a time! And he was at least six feet tall and already twenty! Not a silly teenage boy like the ones she knew at school. She remembered thinking at the time, "If this isn't Love at First Sight, the sky isn't up and the sun doesn't set every night...."

"Sister... Sister!"

The happy bright-eyed sixteen year old "Birthday Girl" looked up through ninety-five year old bloodshot eyes not comprehending where she was. It seemed like whatever they were on was moving but what was it? It didn't look anything like the Art Deco ship called the Ile de France. Where was she? She stared into the concerned eyes of a waitress whose face was quite worn and wrinkled and whose hands shook as she handed her the luncheon meal. Sister accepted the plate smiling slightly even though she had no idea who the woman was or where she came from. She had only managed to eat a few bites of the baked chicken before....

She returned to the Ile de France and her sixteenth birthday celebration the first night out. She was wearing a powder blue full length lace gown her Mother bought for her at an exclusive women's shop in New York City. Oh what a fine feast she enjoyed with her parents and James and his parents! Lobster. Shrimp. Steak. And the pièce de résistance - Baked Alaska!

Father even let her drink a whole glass of champagne when he made a toast to her future. "To my darling Mary, may you grow up to be a fine woman with a very happy life!" Father's normally blue eyes seemed to now have a hint of green. How the pink liquid sparkled and fizzed all the way down her throat! This was so unusual since most of the time Father was so religious disavowing any alcohol or gambling or any violations of the Ten Commandments. But today was his only daughter's special sixteenth birthday party so he made an exception. How great that was for her!

Then something even more fantastic happened. Her charming new friend James asked her to dance a waltz! She felt so totally fine and very grown up in his arms swirling and swirling around the huge ballroom! Later when they walked out on the deck under the dome of stars above the ocean, he held her hand as he told her, "Oh, Mary, you are the loveliest girl I've ever met in my whole life!" She could still feel how hard her heart was pounding at that moment....

Pounding! Vibrating! Roaring! Raucous music assailed Sister Eustacia's ears. Sinatra tunes that had been playing when she and her sister friends got on the boat had been replaced now by the DJ with what she could only describe as "Street Music" that the teenagers obviously liked as their bodies gyrated across the floor to its rhythms. She watched the girl who had grinned at her earlier as she danced but instead saw herself dancing with James but to a different type of music....

They weren't in the Grand Ballroom with their parents waltzing to an eighteen piece orchestra anymore. Now they were in another room dancing to really lively fun music with upbeat rhythms. The Charleston, that's what the dance was called.

"Oh, and my hair's been bobbed! My long hair... is now on the floor. When did that happen? And what is this I'm wearing? A beaded form-fitting Flapper dress like the ones I saw once in a magazine. My stockings are even rolled up and my knees painted red. Imagine! And we're drinking many more glasses of champagne or hooch or giggle water as the Flappers call it."

A few lines of a song she heard that night rushed back into her memory. "Roll 'em, Girls. Roll 'em... Show your pretty knees... Laugh at Ma. Laugh at Pa." How risqué she was feeling though she had no idea how she ever got this way. She just couldn't comprehend how everything happened. She only knew she was feeling so fine and for the first time in her short life wonderfully free as well! She vaguely remembered James telling her how the Flappers got their name because of the way they flapped their arms like birds when they danced the Charleston and now here she was doing the same thing....

The old nun squirmed in her seat on the luncheon cruise. The teenagers in front of her were dancing in very suggestive ways now although some danced solo and some extremely close. Oh they were entirely too close to each other. Father would never have approved of that! Why what they were doing actually looked... what was the word?... obscene... almost like... they were getting ready to... Oh no, they couldn't be!

She had admitted to James she was nervous wondering if her Father would find out everything that she'd been doing that night on the Ile de France, but he reassured her he'd never know where they went for her to change out of her lovely gown into the Flapper dress and all that they did together. He told her she could wear a wig later to hide her short hair, and she could give the dress he borrowed from his sister back to her at the end of the evening.

Oh, what really great fun she and James had dancing together! She adored the Charleston having caught on to how to do it almost immediately. James brought her several more glasses of champagne during breaks. She downed each one almost in one gulp since she was so thirsty.

Too soon the music stopped leaving her feeling very happy though quite off balance and wobbly. She heard James telling her over and over again, "Oh, dear Mary, now that I've found you, I can't ever let you go!" Then he sang his rendition of some lines from a popular song, "I see your smiling face... a fireplace... just you and me and baby makes three... we'll be so happy in our blue heaven." Of course, at the time she could never have imagined the twisted significance those words would have one day.

Without asking her, James took her hand and led her up the stairs to a different floor from hers. At first she didn't want to go into his stateroom with him, but he seemed like such a fine gentleman and she was feeling so free and more than a bit lightheaded by this time that she agreed without a second thought.

Next she remembered James asking her to take off the Flapper dress she liked so much so he could return it to his sister. After that he tickled her until she fell on the bed laughing hysterically. All of a sudden she felt his fingers circling round and round her breasts. She tried to move away, but since it started feeling so strangely good, she stopped squirming. Then he kissed her hard full on the lips. Not a little peck on the cheek like Louis, her friend from school, had given her when she was just a child of ten. No, she was sure this was an adult kiss. After that she stared at James as he took off his pants and even his underwear, but she didn't understand why. Her mind was a foggy road. For the life of her she couldn't comprehend what was happening. Before she took several deep breaths, she felt one of his fingers inching inside her body! Still she really didn't understand what he was doing. She tried to pull away but James kept telling her, "Relax, Mary." Then he released his finger and slipped off her underwear. She tried to protest but apparently not convincingly enough because then she felt something else slip inside her body.

Just as she cried out, "Oh, James!" the stateroom door flew open. Standing there glaring with murderous brown eyes at the two of them in bed was her Father! He charged into the room and grabbed Mary out of James' embrace leaving behind a small pool of blood on the bed. He was swearing so loud she was overwhelmed. She had never seen or heard him so incredibly angry. After he pulled her off the bed, he wrapped her in the top sheet and roughly pushed James on the floor vowing, "If I ever see you with my daughter again, I'll kill you!" Now Mary was more than scared. She was petrified and couldn't move! She was in the middle of a waking nightmare if ever there was one! It was only many days later that she began to realize what really happened that night she turned sixteen....

The loud music kept drumming in Sister Eustacia's ears as the girl who had smiled at her earlier continued dancing across the small dance floor laughing, laughing....

But all Mary could do was cry. Cry when she woke up in the morning. Cry during the day. Cry throughout every evening. Even cry in her sleep. Her Father had disowned her, ranting and raging that his business was going to suffer major losses when his associate found out what she and James did. Then he screamed, "You sinful girl, you will suffer for this!"

If only there had been some way to get in touch with James, but there wasn't. Father made her a prisoner in her room for the rest of the voyage. Stewards delivered her meals though she hardly ate or drank anything for days. She was so flustered and confused nothing would stay down in her stomach. Why was her Father so incredibly angry with her and James? Everything that had happened that one special night became like a ball that kept rolling in many different directions. She couldn't figure out what way it went. That was how she felt about all the events of that night. They were so mixed up in her mind obviously from the effects of all the glasses of champagne she drank sometimes in one gulp that she couldn't have told anyone what came first, second or third. All she knew for certain was the last of them when her Father charged into James' stateroom and threw the two of them out of bed. Oh, her mind and body and soul were so muddled! She couldn't think straight about anything.

She did consider asking one of the stewards to deliver a message to James, though, but changed her mind almost right away realizing that since they were most likely being paid by her Father, they would certainly have to report anything like that she did to him. There was no way she could risk his further wrath.

So she cried and cried until there were ridges in her face like really old ladies had where the tears had streamed down. Cried until she had no energy left to wipe away the tears from her face. Cried until her insides became dried up and shrunken. She just didn't understand all that had happened. What did she do wrong? What did James do wrong? She didn't know what the "crepe" word meant that her Father had whispered to her Mother. Through the fog in her brain and body, she just couldn't remember exactly what she and James had done and why her parents were so angry with him and her....

Sister Eustacia could never forget every scene and every emotion of the most frightening nightmare she ever had the second night she cried herself to sleep locked in her stateroom....

She was dancing the Charleston but not with James. No, with her Father who had horns on his head and a long red tail she kept tripping over! His deep red eyes bore holes right into her heart, but she didn't fall down. She didn't die. Instead she kept asking for more champagne. A waiter who looked exactly like James brought it to her and poured it directly down her throat. It burned so terribly she cried out in agony, but no one was anywhere to come to her assistance. She sat down on the floor trying to rub the red off her knees, but all she saw was blood flowing down her legs. Her Father's voice rang out, "Little Girl, you are damned to Hell!" as he laughed raucously like a madman and picked up a massive bluish jade stone to throw at her....

Mary woke up shaking uncontrollably and sobbing, "Why, Daddy? Why?" She would never dare call him that friendly name to his face, but now it seemed right for some reason. She was already languishing in Hell in this room thanks to him and only he could let her out.

On the third day of her "imprisonment," her Mother ducked into her stateroom but, Mary noted, only after looking up and down the corridor. It occurred to her then that she was afraid of Father, too, even though she had been his wife for nearly a quarter of a century.

"Oh my darling Mary, how very sorry I am about everything that has happened to you!"

"I'm sorry too, Mother. It all happened so fast. Why is Father so angry at me and James?"

"My poor, poor child, it's all my fault! I should have explained some important things to you long before now way before now. I should have...."

"What, Mother? What?"

"Well, you see, my dear... Oh, I don't know where to begin... No one told me or prepared me ahead of time either, but that shouldn't be my excuse. Things didn't have to... You didn't have to be...."

"Oh, Mother, what is it? Please stop crying."

"Oh, my baby, it's not you who should be sorry. It's me. Only me! I should have told you what could happen between a man and a woman when... when...."

"When what, Mother?"

"I can't find the right words, Mary. Let me sit a moment and then I'll try...." The distraught woman's ample body fell down onto the edge of Mary's single bed. After taking several deep breaths, she started over, "You see when a man wants to show his feelings for a woman, he holds her in his arms and touches her at different places on her body. Then his body responds and his manly organ grows and gets hard so he can put it inside the woman where his seed can be released and she can hopefully become a mother nine months later. But this should only happen between two people who are committed to each other in marriage. Otherwise... Oh I should have told you all of this long before now, my baby, but the time was never right. You grew up too fast. I just didn't know what to say to you and now James has done a horrible thing by taking advantage of your innocence. Oh, I'm so sorry, Mary. Please forgive me!" Sobs wracked the woman's body as she stopped talking and looked down at the floor. Guilt like a huge demon had almost sucked the life out of her.

Mary sat astounded, anger welling up in her body. How did she live for sixteen years without knowing what can happen between a man and a woman? Why hadn't someone told her all of this way before now? And that someone should have been her Mother. Her Mother she had relied on and trusted so much for as long as she could remember. Her Mother who was her Mainstay, her Fortress, her Rock when Father was irked or mad or angry with her.

She stared for a long time at her sobbing in front of her for the first time in her life. "Oh, Mother, I'm trying hard to understand. What can I do to make things OK again? And when can I leave here?"

"All I can say, my darling, is that James probably presumed you wanted to...."

"Oh no. I had been drinking many glasses of champagne and... somehow my hair was bobbed, my knees were painted red, I put on someone else's dress, and God knows what else. But how could he think I was...."

"You're just a little girl, Mary. Not aware yet of all the ways of the world. Being with a man that way should only be if you are married to him."

"But why did James do what he did?"

"Well, some men take advantage of certain situations like being with an innocent young girl. It gives them pleasure."

"But why, Mother? Shouldn't the girl or woman feel

pleasure too?"

"Yes, to a certain degree maybe after a while, but not in the same way as a man. James was giving in to his lesser instincts with you. His actions should have been reserved for a woman he loves who is his wife, Mary, not an innocent young girl he just met like you."

"Oh, Mother. I shouldn't have gone to his stateroom that night. Or let him take me dancing in a different part of the ship where I drank more champagne."

"Dear Mary, I'm so sorry you have experienced this at such a young age. That awful boy...."

"Please don't be mad at James, Mother. I...."

"Mary, my darling, remember James is a number of years older than you and should be much wiser. He's the most guilty one and that's it! Only...."

"Only what, Mother? Tell me!"

Sister Eustacia kept repeating, "Tell me! Tell me!" until everyone around her was looking over. After her outburst, it got deathly quiet for a moment before the usual din of the boat returned.

"Well, it's your Father and his temper. He's made some decisions about what you are to do when we get home in several weeks."

"What? How can he do that? How can you let him ruin my life, Mother?"

"Please, Mary. You have to know how much he loves his little girl."

"Oh, Mother, tell me what he wants me to do."

"He made me promise, dear, not to tell you now. At home will be soon enough."

Without another word Mary's Mother tiptoed out of the room, leaving her daughter even more upset. What was her Father going to do? What horrible punishment did he have in mind for her? What a dreadful birthday celebration this was turning out to be!

Oh, how she wished she could talk to James. Why didn't he come to her stateroom? Did her Father have her door watched? After all, he has so much money he can do whatever he chooses. That was the problem. The horrid truth! She was a prisoner on the ship with her Father as her Warden. She couldn't even have any visitors except her Mother and she had to sneak into her room to see her. Oh how much angrier Father would be if he found out she had done that....

Sister Eustacia kept shaking her head back and forth, to and fro. Anyone watching her would have thought she had the palsy....

What an abominable non-vacation her sixteenth birthday cruise had become! The worst thing was that her Father forbade her to leave her stateroom. She felt so utterly forlorn and forsaken.

Chapter 2

A Mother's Compassion

Caught between two birthday celebrations eighty years apart, Sister continued to bob and shake her head. The teenage girl who had grinned at her earlier noticed her strange movements and wondered what she was thinking. Since she was so ancient, she just figured it was some kind of malady old people - especially old lady nuns - suffered.

There was no way the teen could have ever even imagined the overwhelming experiences Sister Eustacia was reliving in her memory as her head flowed repeatedly from right to left under her crooked headpiece and veil. Sister felt almost sick now watching the cavorting teenagers on the small dance floor.

Oh, Father would certainly never have approved of the ways they were dancing! Why it almost looked like they were actually starting to... except they were standing up....

Sister felt someone pulling at her wheelchair. She turned to see one of the teenage girls who volunteered at the retirement home standing by her side asking if she needed a bathroom break. Sister Eustacia shook her head yes, glad for a few minutes respite from the grating sounds of the loud music and the offensive sight of the young adults dancing so wildly and especially from her Father's anger and her profound nervousness about what he planned for her when they got home from their vacation abroad....

The small bathroom on board the luncheon cruise seemed about the size of the one in her stateroom on the Ile de France where she was now sitting on the commode feeling extremely depressed and alone. Who said a taste of pleasure was better than nothing? Only one more awful day and then at least she could get out of this room and off this ship! But what would happen to her then? What would her Father tell her she had to do in Paris? Would he allow her to go sightseeing? Or would he insist she be kept under lock and key in her room there too?

She cried out, "Oh no! Oh no!"

"Sister Eustacia, are you OK?"

"Oui, je suis fantastique!"

"What did you say, Sister? I didn't understand you."

"Pas de problem. Je suis fantastique!"

At that the elderly nun knocked on the stall door for the aide to come in to help her get back into her wheelchair. She peered all around the boat as she was wheeled back to her place at the table. For a long moment she didn't know where she was again. However, when the raucous music assailed her ears once more and she saw the teens still dancing in their seductive ways, she realized she hadn't arrived in Paris with her parents yet.

She worried about where her Father would decide she had to stay there. Would he insist she still be a prisoner in her room? Would he continue to punish her so unfairly for what she so innocently let happen on her sixteenth birthday? Probably. Her knees felt so sore, chafed from her scrubbing the red paint off them. The wig her Mother made her wear itched terribly. She wanted to rip it off her head and let the whole world see that she had bobbed her hair, but she knew she'd get in a lot more trouble with her Father if she did. He absolutely abhorred short hair. How furious he was when he saw hers! Of course, he blamed James for that too.

Poor James. Mary wished she could talk to him somehow. She wondered if he was going to Paris too. If Father let her do some sightseeing, maybe she'd run into him by accident. But what would she say to him? Would she tell him she was angry at what he had done to her and blame him for her punishment? Would she ever even want to let him touch her again? Would he want her again the way he had her on the boat? She shivered and frowned as she wondered.

"Sister, Sister, what's the matter? You look so upset!"

"I'm all right, thank you. Don't worry. I'll find a way to make it through all of this."

"What are you talking about, Sister Eustacia?"

"No, that's not my name. My name's Mary. Things have to change when we get to Paris. Mother Elias will take care of me. She's been more my Mother than... She would have told me things I should have known in advance... She wouldn't have waited until it was too late... after what happened.... Oh James, if only...."

The young aide rolled her eyes. Then she remembered the old nun's problem with her confused mind though she could never have guessed where the Paris, Mother Elias and James connections came from. Earlier she had talked to one of the old nun's friends enjoying the cruise when they both walked out on the upper deck to enjoy the view of the boats on the water and see Fort McHenry.

"Sister Joseph, I was wondering... I mean... I don't understand something. What's the matter with Sister Eustacia? I never know what to say to her."

"Oh, Julie, it's really so sad. We think Sister's experiencing the effects of a terrible disease called Alzheimer's. You've already noticed how she's here one minute and somewhere else the next. That's one of the main indicators of that condition."

"How long has she been this way, Sister?"

"I'm not sure, Julie. Many years ago we more or less grew up together in the convent. You see, we entered as teenagers around the same time and became soul sisters, but the community sent us separate ways over the years so I really didn't see much of Sister until I ended up at Saint Clara's Retirement Home with her about fifteen years ago."

"Was Sister's mind OK then?"

"Yes, pretty much but sometimes I'd hear her say things like 'No, she couldn't have died!' or 'Why didn't she tell me?' or 'Why did he leave me?' But that's not important now. We all just try to be there for her as much as possible because lately she's become more and more depressed and distressed. Please understand that whatever she says is simply the ramblings of a person whose mind is partly unhinged."

"That's what I've been trying to do, Sister Joseph. Thanks for filling in some more of the pieces of the puzzle of her behavior for me."

"Let's go back down with everyone now, Julie. You are a good person for wanting to understand Sister. She'll probably need your help again soon."

When the two returned, the DJ was spinning Sinatra's classic "I Did It My Way" as the group of teens left the area to go down to a lower level for a special activity.

As the lines, "Regrets, I've had a few// But then again, too few to mention// I did what I had to do// And saw it through without exception.... I faced it all and I stood tall// And did it my way," coursed through Sister Eustacia's mind, she and her parents arrived at their hotel in Paris. They went to their rooms to rest after the long train ride, but Mary decided to slip out of her room when she was sure her parents were asleep. She had been cooped up in what increasingly seemed like a jail cell on the ship for months as far as she was concerned. She just had to breathe some fresh air.

As soon as she wandered into the ornate lobby, her eyes widened in disbelief. James was standing at the counter registering with his parents! She really wanted to talk to him, but then again she didn't. Before she could decide either way, she heard him call out her name.

"Oh, Mary! Mary! Isn't this a wonderful coincidence? I'm so glad you're here!" Mary felt his blue-green eyes as he looked at her.

"I don't think my Father would like it if he saw us together."

"I know he's an extremely stern man, Mary, but I have to talk to you. I never got a chance on the ship to tell you some things. I'm so sorry."

"But, James, there was no way you could have talked to me because my Father made me a prisoner in my stateroom the whole time and probably had my door watched so no one could come in. Even my Mother had to look down the hall to see if he saw her before she slipped in my room. Oh, this has been so perfectly horrible!"

"Mary, I'm so sorry for everything that's happened. I never meant to hurt you!"

"But I did let you..."

"No, it was all my fault. I shouldn't have let you drink all those glasses of champagne. It wasn't your fault at all, Mary."

"Oh, James!"

"I'm so glad to see you again, Mary. Maybe we can go sightseeing here together."

"Oh no, James, my Father will never let me go out with you. Actually he's forbidden me to see you. And you know what he told you that night he found us."

"He threatened to kill me."

"But James, the only way I'm even here now is I slipped out of my room while my parents were sleeping."

"Well, if worse comes to worse, maybe you can do that again."

"Do what again, young man!? Do what!? Take advantage of my daughter once more!? I told you on the ship that you were never to see her again yet here you are. I erroneously thought we could keep this whole affair quiet for both of our families' sakes, but now I know differently. I should call the authorities immediately and report you for violating my innocent daughter!"

Mary's Father stood ramrod before the two young people,

his furious eyes registering a change from blue to brown. Mary knew that meant even greater consequences for them but especially for her.

"Oh, Father, please don't do that to James. Please don't!"

"You have no say whatsoever in any of this, young lady! Return to your room immediately and remain there until I decide otherwise!" He glared at his daughter now with a resolute fury she had never witnessed in him before.

As Mary reluctantly turned to leave, she smiled weakly at James. What did her Father say to him afterwards? Did he threaten him further? Did he actually report him to the police? Did he tell his parents that he had taken advantage of his daughter? The worst of it was she never saw James again. Apparently, her Father made quite certain of that! Maybe he even paid him to stay away from her.

Again Sister Eustacia sat shaking her head and shivering. Why didn't she ever find out what happened to James all those years ago?

She remembered throwing herself on her bed sobbing uncontrollably when she got back to her room that terrible day. She didn't know how much time passed before she heard a firm knock on her door. She jumped up wiping her eyes, vowing her Father would not see any of her tears. He stormed into the room quickly looking all around as though he thought she might have stashed James away somewhere under the bed or in the large closet. Mary shivered not knowing what to expect...

"Would you like a shawl for over your shoulders, Sister Eustacia? You look cold," her concerned aide asked.

"Indeed, I am very cold, Julie. Cold to the bones of me. Cold and so afraid."

"Afraid of what, Sister?"

"Of him. My Father."

"But why? Your Father in Heaven loves you."

"Not him. My Father here on Earth who's determined to control my life. I wouldn't be... if he hadn't...."

"What, Sister? If he hadn't what?"

"Well, I don't know. He hasn't told me yet. I'm scared. So scared! I don't know what to expect."

The elderly nun closed her eyes pulling the proffered shawl around her shaking shoulders. Her aide, thinking she was going to take a spur of the moment cat nap, left her side to take a short walk on the deck. Actually, she couldn't wait to get away from the old nun she was in charge of. She just never knew whether she was in the here and now or somewhere else. It was all so confusing. She really hoped she'd never end up that way. Actually, it wasn't fair that some people got old like this. She remembered her Grandma was "out of it" too when she was in her eighties. It was so sad to try to talk to her when she didn't even know who she really was. One day her mind was so confused that she called her by her Mother's name.

In the meantime Sister Eustacia's disjointed memory pulled her to travel back to the Paris hotel. Her Father stood over her glaring with his now big brown eyes almost bulging out of his head. "Fury" was written in scowling lines across his face. Mary couldn't imagine what he was going to say or do, but he didn't make her wait more than a few seconds to find out.

"Mary, you have continued to defy me by going against my expressed directions! Your behavior has been and continues to be utterly unacceptable and out of control so you must be punished accordingly. I believed initially that forbidding you to leave your stateroom on the Ile de France would have been adequate, but apparently you still insist on defying me by refusing to follow my explicit directions. Since you left your room without my permission and arranged to see that poor excuse of a man in full view of everyone in the lobby no less, you have incurred my added wrath!"

Mary cringed thinking her Father was about to hit her, but for some reason she couldn't comprehend he didn't. Instead, he simply stood glaring down at her, his eyes like nails being pounded into her body. That felt worse than if he had jerked off his leather belt and beaten her until she bled.

"But, Father, I just needed some fresh air. I saw James in the lobby quite by chance. I didn't even know his family was staying in this hotel too."

"Do you honestly expect me to believe that story, you

disobedient girl? Can you be that ignorant?"

"But, Father!"

"I don't want to hear another word out of you, you sinful child! Close your mouth and listen very carefully to what I'm going to tell you."

"Yes, Father. Yes, Father. Yes, Father."

The elderly nun kept repeating her answer across eight decades. The other nuns and the aides sitting around her could only turn away embarrassed at her apparent flow in and out of reality. Though they tried to ignore her, they knew all too well the difficulties their fellow sister was having with her mind and memory. They also knew there was no way they could really help her. At best all they could do was try to accept and humor her. They had initially believed that a day away from the Home - an excursion to celebrate her birthday would help her out of her doldrums at least for a short time, but as the afternoon passed, they realized that something on this cruise had upset her to the point that she was apparently in a worse state here on the boat than in her room at Saint Clara's.

The waitress named Naomi tottered over to their table in the next few minutes with Sister Eustacia's two-layered birthday cake. She had put ten candles on it ready to be lit, one for each decade of the nun's life.

Sister Eustacia counted the candles. Then her face became extremely contorted as she screamed at the waitress,

"You've left off six candles! There should be sixteen on the cake! Mother and especially Father will be very upset if you don't add them and so will I! Hurry! There must be sixteen candles on my birthday cake!"

"I'm so sorry, Sister," the waitress purred, not understanding the old nun's problem. "I'll get the extra candles right away," she mumbled shaking her gray head.

Before the other nuns at the table could stop her, Naomi hobbled back across the length of the boat and returned with six additional candles. Sister Eustacia clapped her hands gleefully like a little girl who's just been given a special present as the waitress added them to the cake and then lit all sixteen with a lighter she pulled out of her pants' pocket. Then everyone sang "Happy Birthday, Sister!" as huge tears flowed freely down the nun's weathered face.

As she ate her birthday cake, the sweetness of the chocolate icing startled her as she said to no one in particular, "I really like sweet things. I would have nicknamed my little girl 'Sweetness.'"

Her mind flipped back then to the month before she delivered her baby. As the little one seemed to kick gleefully inside her body, the reality of her impending situation overwhelmed her. Why had she been so out of it, not finding out what was going to happen to her baby once it was born? Of course, she had to leave the convent to raise it, but her Mother's dying wish was for her to "stay a good nun." When was that? Before or after all of this happened? She couldn't be sure. How could she be a good Mother and a good nun at the same time?

Her mind clouded with uncertainty and overflowing with unanswered questions, she knew she had to talk to someone. Sadly, though, she realized there was no one. No one! Oh, if only Mother Elias were still alive. If only she were here, she'd know what to do.

"Mother Elias. Mother Elias," she called out suddenly.

"Who, Sister? Mother Elias? No one by that name is with us today," her aide responded.

Sister Eustacia stared at the other nuns and their aides at the table. Where had they come from? Why were they each eating pieces of her sixteenth birthday cake? Were they her parents' friends on the big ship across the ocean or simply strangers who crashed her special party? For the life of her trembling hands, she couldn't decide. All she knew was that she wanted another piece of her cake. "More cake. More cake. More cake," she kept mumbling. Her aide cut her a slice of what she was going to take home to her boyfriend. Sister ate it almost in one bite.

Ah, chocolate. Chocolate and James! Why was she thinking about him now? Oh yes, he offered her some chocolate during their few hours together. For once in her life then she had refused the sweet treat gulping down another big taste of the sparkling champagne instead.

But where was James now? Had he left the ship? Sister peered all around the table where she was sitting with her fellow nuns. He wasn't there. Then she peered all around the ship but he wasn't there either. She even looked under the table thinking he was playing some kind of weird joke on her. He wasn't anywhere....

Oh, but then she looked up into his splendid blue-green eyes. He was on top of her for some reason. And neither of them were wearing any clothes! She shivered again down to her bones when her Father burst into the room....

"What's happening to me?" she asked herself. "Why do I have this black thing on my head and these odd clothes on my body? Where's my long blue sweet sixteen gown my Mother bought me? Oh where am I?"

She wondered if she could relive the rest of her sixteenth birthday. For a few fleeting moments she really believed she could change everything, but then a flash of reality from the past came back to her like a big gulp of sour milk. She swallowed trying to get rid of the disgusting taste of bile in her mouth.

"Yes, Father!" kept hammering through her brain. He was still glaring at her now no matter how many times she repeated them. Then he bellowed, "Quiet, Mary! I have some very important words to say to you. Listen very carefully. I have decided that you do not deserve this vacation since you defied me again and talked to that scoundrel James. You have sinned seriously against the Fourth Commandment, Mary, and also violated the Sixth Commandment when you got in bed with that terrible young man!"

Mary wanted to protest with her whole heart and soul but knew if she dared there would be more hell to pay than she could stand. Instead she forced herself to bite her lip and stay silent as her Father continued raging at her.

"So, Mary, since you have persisted in disobeying me and God, I have taken steps for your own good to force you to do penance for your transgressions. Now it is your duty to prove to Almighty God and to me that you are truly sorry for your sins. To do this, here in Paris you are again forbidden to leave your room unless it is to go with your Mother and me to the Cathedral of Notre Dame for Confession and Mass. Otherwise you are to spend your time in this room reading the Bible which I have especially purchased for you for this purpose. Furthermore, I expect you to summarize what you read each day and then write down the lessons you have learned from those lines. I will come to your room each evening to pick up your writing. Only then will your dinner be brought to you."

Mary was never so dumbfounded in her whole young life! Had she really heard what she thought she heard? Did her Father really go off the deep end to punish her to this extreme just because she accidentally ran into James in the hotel lobby?

Before she could chance a reaction to his declaration, he stormed out of her room. It struck Mary that he left like that before he changed his mind or did something worse like lash out to her with his clenched fists.

The weeks dragged on for Mary at a sick snail's pace. She knew her survival depended on doing the assignment her Father gave her so she sloshed through the reading and writing with a determined reluctance. One day she read The Gospel of Saint John - the part about the Last Supper. It really spoke to her particularly when Jesus told his Apostles, "You now indeed have sorrow, but I will see you again and your heart shall rejoice and your joy no man shall take from you." Across the decades it was as though James was saying those reassuring words to her. And, of course, the last line had to refer to her Father taking away all her fun. Naturally, though, she didn't dare write this in the lesson of the day for him to read. Instead she just wrote cryptically, "Jesus promised his men that they'd be happy again when he came back. Probably he was alluding to his Resurrection." Each evening she handed writing like this to her Father as the waiter brought in her dinner tray....

The table in front of her now was being cleared. The wrinkled waitress smiled at her every time she picked up some unused cutlery or dishes....

The next thing she knew she herself was clearing tables as well. But where? Nothing looked familiar. This certainly was not a regular restaurant. Why would she, the only daughter of an extremely wealthy man who could afford the cost of tickets for three ocean liner trips across the Atlantic on the most expensive ship at sea as well as three two week stays at an exclusive hotel in Paris, be cleaning up strangers' dinner dishes? It didn't make any sense at all. Again her mind was so clouded she nearly cried out loud in total terror, "Where am I? How did I get wherever this place is? Why am I wearing this ugly long black skirt and....?"

Suddenly, with a powerful awareness that hit her like a thousand devastating punches in her stomach, it all came back to her. Her holier-than-thou Father had forced her to enter a convent in Baltimore, Maryland, of all places in the world, so far from home that none of her friends and certainly not James would ever know where to find her!

How did she let this happen? How did he actually make her become a nun locked away from the world? Away from men. And marriage. And babies. And from any kind of an ordinary life! Why couldn't she remember everything that led to her coming here? Could she have been drugged? Didn't anyone ask her if she came of her own free will? Or did her Father bribe the Mother Superior of the Community with a large amount of money to put her in this place? "Money talks with a very loud voice," he always used to say. All these questions kept pounding relentlessly on the door of her brain.

As she stood staring into space hoping answers would

unlock the door, someone nudged her saying very softly, "Sister Mary, hurry! We have to finish here as soon as we can. Otherwise we'll be late for chapel and then Mother Superior will give us a big penance."

Mary remembered then how sick to her stomach she felt in the early days every time she had to kneel on the floor by the side of Mother Elias' desk to ask for a penance for talking after the Grand Silence at nine o'clock each night or breaking a dish in the refectory or for some other transgression she usually considered meaningless like not getting permission to wash her hair. She hurried to finish her assigned work so she wouldn't be subjected to that again. At least not today.

As soon as she knelt down in the chapel, thankfully a full five minutes early, the occurrences of the past few months came back to her with a palpable rush of emotion that nearly knocked her out of the pew. Her Father, that vindictive, self righteous Old Man, hell bent on punishing her to the hilt for what she let James do, made her give her life away!

She also recalled, though, that it was her loving Mother's pleas that softened the blow. "How had she been brave enough to challenge him?" she wondered many years later. Yes, it was her dear Mother who had insisted that Mary should be permitted to decide whether she wanted to leave or not after the twelve months she had to stay behind convent walls, cut off from the world with no idea of what was going on out there. With no pleasures. Only austerities and denials of her basic self and womanhood. And penance and more penance. Prayers and more prayers. Work and more work. A strange world full of odd rules like having to get permission to go to the attic where their trunks were to retrieve her winter cloaks.

How was she going to survive here after all she was used to for all her life - all she took for granted in her other life? She missed her Mother so much. And unbelievably to her, even to a slight degree her self-righteous Father though on some level of her psyche, she was relieved to be far away from him, one of the good things of being stuck in this place. Still it was so unfair that he arranged, probably with a big donation to the Community, for her to come here. That Vindictive, Conniving, Sanctimonious Old Man!

Sister Mary's stomach growled. She felt very hungry but not only for the food so carefully rationed at every meal that she never felt completely satisfied. No, she was starved more for care. For affection. For the smile of an understanding person. For inner feelings of self esteem instead of the constant denigration of herself. Not for constant soul searching for trivial violations of the Rule. Or daily Examinations of Conscience at noon in Chapel and weekly Confession with no real sins to tell the priest. Or worse, monthly admissions of her faults in front of the chapel to the whole Community. "I accuse myself before God and you my sisters...." of whatever insignificant departure from the Rule that the Mother Superior had decided she should announce to everyone.

She remembered now that she was what the nuns called a postulant having been in their midst for only a few months though it seemed like centuries since the night of her sixteenth birthday. She recalled now it had only been ten weeks. Not even three months. How she missed her other life! How many nights had she cried herself to sleep in her narrow white-sheeted single bed in her long white cotton nightgown wishing she could be with James again or with one of her close girlfriends or with her dear Mother. She was surrounded by other nuns her age in the dorm room with thick curtains giving each some privacy, but she still felt like she was shipwrecked all alone on a desert island with no hope of rescue.

She'd been sick at heart and stomach almost from Day One, feeling so forsaken and separated from everyone she loved. Almost every morning she threw up in the six stalled bathroom fortunately, she thought, before the other new nuns woke up and came in to use its shared facilities. Many other mornings at breakfast she felt queasy having to spoon hot syrupy raisins which she loathed onto her plate since they were required to eat some of whatever was served at every meal. She never used to detest eating these black blobs as much in the past, but now she had to summon every ounce of control in her body to restrain herself from regurgitating all over the table into the areas where her fellow sisters sat in a row eating most of the time, of course, in silence. Then just yesterday morning she had to fly out of chant class suddenly and almost didn't make it to the bathroom in time.

After chapel Sister Mary walked down the long, always highly polished corridor to the sewing room for a class the new nuns were to have on how to run the treadle machines to sew their habits and headpieces. On the way she happened to glance at the blackboard outside Mother Superior's office. Her name was sprawled in large letters across it! One of the older nuns called novices had told her what that meant. She was in some kind of Big Trouble!

Between the class and lunch she managed to get up all her courage to knock on Mother Elias' door. "Come in, Sister Mary," the ancient-to-her older woman said.

"I saw my name on the blackboard, Mother. May I have my penance for whatever I've done wrong?"

"Oh, I'm sorry, Sister. When I sprawl a name on the board, I know some of you think that Sister has violated the Rule so I'm sending for her to give her some sort of punishment. Today I was just in a big hurry when I wrote yours since I was so anxious to ask how you're doing, Sister." The older nun searched the young nun's eyes noting they were brown with a hint of green.

"OK, Mother. That is, I mean I'm doing fine."

"No, I don't think you are, Sister Mary. Several of the sisters have told me about your frequent bathroom visits. They have even heard you throwing up in the morning and seen you almost running to the bathroom on a number of occasions. I'm very concerned about you, Sister, so I've set up an appointment with Dr. Vincent for you at our hospital in the city. We need to find out why you're having these problems. Why your stomach is so often upset."

"But maybe it's just the different food I've been eating, Mother, that's upsetting my stomach. Food I'm not used to. I'll be all right."

"No, Sister Mary, I sense it's something more serious than that. Your appointment is at 2 o'clock tomorrow afternoon. Sister Ramona will be your companion. A taxi will pick the two of you up at 12:30." Sister remembered that the nuns of her Community didn't drive then.

So Mary's whole life started to change again. Mother Elias knew something.

Chapter 3

A Daughter's Trauma

How could she have ever known what Dr. Vincent would determine was the cause of her problems. As they sat in a windowless private room with bare white walls, he simply said, "Sister, you're with child."

Stunned beyond belief, Mary could only sit, mouth agape in shock, for many minutes. How could this be? She never seriously considered how women became "with child." Did she somehow get this way from that one fleeting encounter with James?

What would Mother Superior say when she told her? Worse, what would her parents, especially her Father, do when they found out? She had been essentially under lock and key ever since their one time together. Would James be safe from the

41

wrath of her Father? How she wished there was some way she could get in touch with him herself first, but she knew there was no hope that she could especially here in this place where she was effectively cut off from the world. She didn't have any access to a telephone even if she knew how to reach him. Furthermore, she had no money and never any privacy. She might as well have been lost on a desert island for how isolated she was from the world she used to know.

Scraps of a conversation came back to her out of the antiseptic smell of the consultation room. Apparently, she had pushed the disturbing memory so far back into a corner of her brain that she only vaguely recalled hearing her Father threatening James after he found him talking to her in the hotel lobby. She had defied his orders to go straight back to her room and had hidden behind a huge pillar nearby instead listening to the two of them.

Her Father's restrained anger scared her to the tips of her toe nails even though she could only make out certain key words. "You filthy... I could kill... a proposition... get lost... never.... again.... $2500... university...."

Mary watched in horror as James grabbed a check out of her Father's hand. She expected him to rip it up in his face then, but he simply jammed it in his pocket and strolled away! Rivers of tears blinding her eyes, Mary ran to her room in total incredulity. Her James let himself be bought off by her Father?

Why? Why? Didn't he really care about her as he said he did? Or was he so afraid of her Father like everyone else, even her Mother and certainly her. "Oh why, James? Why did you take his blackmail money?" Mary wailed in her head to the walls of her room....

Then she very calmly asked the doctor, "Are you absolutely sure I'm with child, Dr. Vincent?"

"Yes, unfortunately, I am, Sister Mary. You are now more than two months along."

Along. Alone. Lonely. Distraught. Depressed. Sister Mary ran out of the doctor's office. Refusing to tell her sister companion what was the matter, she choked back sobs all the way home to the Novitiate floor of the Motherhouse where she saw her name on the blackboard once more, this time in small letters. Holding herself very carefully in check, she knocked on the Mother Superior's door.

"Please come in, Sister, and close the door behind you." Mary knew she was really in for it now. No other nun met with Mother Elias behind a closed door.

"So, Sister Mary, you saw Dr. Vincent today."

"Yes, Mother. He told me I'm...."

"Yes, I know, Sister. He called to tell me as soon as he determined it."

"Oh, Mother Elias, I didn't realize what was happening when... I mean and I didn't know I could get this way the first time in just a few minutes... My parents and I were on a big boat to France to celebrate my sixteenth birthday. Father introduced me to James, the son of one of his business associates. He was so handsome and had these beautiful blue-green eyes. Oh, we had such fun dancing and drinking champagne! I got my hair bobbed and put on his sister's Flapper dress and even painted my knees red. Then James took me to his stateroom and he... we... Oh, Mother Elias, I'm sorry... I...." At this point all of Mary's resolves to stay calm disintegrated as she put her head down on the older woman's desk and cried in wrenching sobs....

Sister Eustacia's face was a waterfall of tears as everyone started to prepare to leave the boat. She knew she was very sad and crying as a result but couldn't remember for the life of her why. What was happening to her? Why was she crying for no apparent reason? Why was everyone at the table looking away from her in the other direction? What was the matter with her? With no answers forthcoming, the elderly nun let herself swim in the raging waters of her overwhelming emotions....

She was pregnant. With child! James was going to be a Father and there was no way to tell him. And there was more. She was going to be a Mother! From her disjointed memory she heard Mother Elias announce, "Sister Mary, I've decided that the best thing for you now is to go away. To leave us."

"Leave here, Mother? Oh, my Father won't hear of it! He's insisted that I have to stay in this convent for at least a year to do penance for my sins. Oh, Mother Elias, I just can't leave now. Father won't let me. He is such a terribly stern and vindictive man!"

"But, Sister, you must understand that in your present condition, you simply cannot remain here. You will disedify everyone when you start to show. How could you deal with that? And what's more, what would that do to the Community's image? No, I'm sorry, Sister Mary, but you simply cannot stay with us in your present condition."

"But, Mother, isn't there some other way? Please I'm begging you. I absolutely cannot go home."

"Well, Sister, actually there is one other possibility. We have a group of nuns who run a home for unwed Mothers in Pennsylvania. You could go there until you have your baby if that's what you want."

"But how will I ever tell my parents especially my Father about this?"

"You won't and I won't. I will simply inform them that we're sending you away for a number of months for special study without any visitors to distract you. That way he and your Mother will never know about your condition and whatever happens as a result in the next seven months."

"Thank you, Mother Elias. I'll go to that place, but what will happen to my baby once it's born?"

"God and I will decide that when the time comes, Sister

Mary. Right now you need to pack. Be at the side door when the cab comes tomorrow morning at 7 a.m. One last thing, Sister, you must not tell anyone about any of this, not even one of the sisters. And you dare not call your parents either before you leave since there's a chance they'll suspect something. Now go in peace, Sister Mary. Hopefully, I'll see you back here within the year."

"Good bye, Mother Elias. Thank you for being so kind and understanding."

As she left her Superior's office, she noticed Mother Elias turn and sit staring out the window. She didn't know she was feeling sad for her and everything she had yet to endure.

Mary arrived at the home and was simply introduced to the other women as just that. No one needed to know she was a new nun. For the next more than half a year, she lived in a kind of cocoon hardly talking to the other "unweds." She preferred staying in her tiny single room by herself most of the time instead. Loneliness took on new meaning to her there. She had no telephone or letter writing privileges. For all intents and purposes, she was more cut off from the world than she had been back in the convent. At least there she could write letters to her parents and see them once a month on Visiting Sundays except during Advent and Lent. It was even worse here than being locked up in her stateroom on the Ile de France. Here she felt more forlorn and forgotten surrounded by strangers in her same predicament who were wrapped up tight in their own situations.

She had no idea what was going to happen to her in the next weeks and months. The future was a blank page in a foreign language book she couldn't read.

Still she knew she couldn't stay in her room all the time as she would have preferred under the circumstances, terrible as they were for her to deal with, because in addition to required meals together, all the "girls" were required to attend special sessions once a week which Mary referred to in her mind as SBA's or "Spiritual Brainwashing Attempts." They usually began with one of the obese old nuns who ran the place standing up in front of the twenty or so in the group, which ranged in age from teens like her to ones she considered very old at thirty. The woman's talk would vary little because that was all she knew from her own limited experience or because there were so many change-overs as the "girls" had their babies and left and others took their places. "Now, girls, you have made certain decisions that have brought you here. You've done reprehensible acts that should be reserved only for those who are married. Pray to God to forgive you your sins and take care of the products of them. It is now for you and God to come to terms with what you have so sinfully chosen to do...."

Without warning for Mary, the nun's strident voice would become her Mother's informing her again of the facts of life in her stateroom on the Ile de France and then lecturing her. "Mary, you must resolve to change your ways now that you have given into this major temptation of the world and are being forced by your Father to deal with the consequences of your decision. You see, there are those out there who have little concern about God's laws because they are addicted to their own pleasures. You must never let them lead you to give in to those same pleasures again until you are married. You must stay strong, my dear. Pray to God to help and sustain you...."

Mary's days at the home passed slowly at first and then towards the end of the seven months slower than a clogged up drain. She really didn't know what to expect at delivery except a nurse told her she would be put under when the time came. Throughout the months in her immaturity and uncertainty about her situation, it never occurred to her to ask anyone again what was going to happen to her baby. Actually, she became increasingly afraid to ask the brusque old nun in charge anything.

She sat watching puffy new snowflakes fall outside her room. It was only much later that she understood why she never had any classes about how to take care of a newborn. In fact, she almost couldn't believe she was about to give birth to one at all. That is, until her stomach bulged out of her dresses more and more each day and then from about the sixth month on, she could feel odd flutters of movements inside her....

Sister Eustacia felt them still now sometimes so many years later. It was like her stomach rebelled to having food in it, especially meat. Since today she had eaten a few bites of the chicken served at lunch, flatulence kept ringing out of her body. Finally, she turned her head in her lopsided headpiece to the aide next to her and whispered, "Please, I need another bathroom break, Julie my dear."

The girl jumped up quickly and wheeled the old nun to the bathroom. Sister felt like her insides were ready to fall out into the toilet somewhat like she felt the night when she went into labor. Then the nun/midwife had held her hand as she was put under remembering her nightmare from the night before....

Her Father was a raging fire about to consume her and James an anorexic rabbit struggling to get her away from him. And all she could do was cry loud screeching wails that woke her dead parents who ran out to her pleading, "Here let us help you, Honey." Then they sat on her stomach smashing it flat baby and all....

It was March 21st, the first day of Spring, when Mary came to after the delivery. She heard a tiny cry and jerked up in her bed screaming, "Where's my baby? I want my baby. Please, Sister, let me hold my baby!"

The nun at her bedside took Mary's shaking hand and held it lovingly. "I'm so sorry, my dear, your daughter has gone to Heaven. She was born dead."

"That can't be! I felt her moving inside me yesterday and I just heard her cry. She can't be!"

"You must accept God's will, my dear. Obviously, he wanted your baby girl for himself. You must pray now for the strength to go on..."

"No, I can't! I won't! I want my baby. I need her right now!"

"Mary you have to calm down. You'll be staying here for several more days to rest. Otherwise your body will not heal properly."

"I don't care! I just want my baby. Where is she? I want to hold her. Please! Please!!"

Mary continued begging and crying hysterically after the nun left her room. Then suddenly, she was struck bone quiet as she overheard two nurses talking outside her door.

"So sad, isn't it? That young girl losing her baby."

Mary tried to call out to them, but her words came out as only tiny peeps so no one heard her. She sank back in bed defeated trying to tell herself she only imagined what she had heard or that the two nurses were talking about some other girl who lost her baby....

After Sister Eustacia finished her business in the bathroom, Julie wheeled her back to the table. On the way Sister noticed the waitress with the wrinkled face standing over by the window apparently taking a break. There was something about her.

All at once, she was back on the Ile de France as James

looked deeply into her eyes. His were so blue, so green as his fingers circled her breasts and then moved to....

The old nun squirmed around in her wheelchair. An awareness almost connected her past with her present memory....

She was on her knees scrubbing the floor of the huge kitchen at the Motherhouse. She couldn't remember if this was before or after her baby daughter supposedly died.

"Sister, Mother Superior wants to see you right away!"

The young nun got up from the floor, washed her hands and hurried off to Mother Elias' office worried she had violated the Rule again in some way she wasn't aware of. She steeled herself for another penance like saying the rosary with her arms outstretched.

She crept into the office as she said softly, "Mother, you sent for me."

"Yes, my dear. Please come over and sit beside me. You've been on your knees in the kitchen for too long."

Sister Mary sat down in the lone other chair in the room eyeing her Superior cautiously.

"Now, Sister Mary, since you've returned from 'your studies,' I've noted that you are extremely unhappy. Is there anything I can do to help you through this difficult time?"

"No, Mother, there isn't. I'm so depressed thinking about my baby I was told died. I can't believe she was stillborn as they said. I felt her growing inside me, Mother. She wasn't dead. She kept kicking me as if to say, 'Here I am getting ready to come out to meet you.'"

The young nun patted her stomach slowly. Her Superior was momentarily at a loss for words. The two sat silent for many minutes. Finally, the older nun found her voice again.

"Sister, I permitted you to return to us after you finished 'your studies' because your Father expected you to stay here for a full year before he would let you decide whether you want to stay here for good or not. Now I'm not sure this plan has been a good idea. I think you should go home now."

"Oh no, please, Mother Elias, I just can't! At least not yet. I can't face my Mother and certainly not my Father! I'm so afraid I'll be weak and break down and tell them everything about their granddaughter who supposedly died. I don't want to even imagine how they'll react although my Father will probably renounce you and me and the whole Community for lying to him. As a result he won't give the Community the thousands of dollars he told me he promised you for your building fund. Then my Mother will collapse and not be able to stop crying. She might even have a nervous breakdown."

"Oh my dear Sister Mary, I don't know what to tell you. If you think you must remain here until your year is up, then I'll honor your decision."

"Oh, I can't thank you enough for understanding me and my situation, Mother. I know if my daughter's really dead, she's in Heaven looking down on me and helping me to try harder to deal with my depression over losing her. Somehow I'll find a way to go on."

There was no way Sister Mary could ever have known what the older nun was thinking as she looked lovingly at her sitting beside her now on the verge of tears. In a parallel universe she could have been her own daughter if she had accepted her teenage boyfriend's offer of marriage instead of giving herself to God when she was about Mary's age. Peter had argued with her that he needed her and that she could save her soul in the world. But she was adamant. She truly believed she had a vocation so three weeks after her eighteenth birthday, she entered the Community.

Of course, there wouldn't have been any chance she could have gotten pregnant and had Peter's child when she was a teenager like poor Sister Mary. At most she and Peter had only hugged and kissed though he had always wanted more and couldn't understand why she kept refusing his advances. Brainwashing with threats of mortal sin and hell and damnation for violation of the Sixth Commandment by the priests and nuns during her twelve years in Catholic schools had kept her from letting him touch her beyond a quick kiss or hug. She recalled the terrible agony she went through after she even let him give her a brief glancing kiss on her lips. Then she'd have to wait in pain until she could go to Confession to tell it to the priest so she wouldn't go to Hell if she was killed or died suddenly.

Out of the blue from many years ago, she heard her Mother tell her and her younger sister when they started dating, "Just don't let him touch your breasts." As though if the guy didn't do that, he wouldn't do anything else. She smiled at the innocent falsehood of that admonition. Still some days when she felt particularly lonely and yearning for a man's physical attentions, she thought about her first and only real boyfriend. Sometimes she wondered what would have happened if she had married Peter as he wanted or what would have happened if...no, that was inexplicable...still what if she had gotten pregnant like this poor young girl in front of her? What if in a moment of weakness she had let her guard down and he had...No, she couldn't imagine it anymore than she could imagine telling her parents, "Oh, I just found out I'm going to have a baby."

What would they have done with so little money and such a small two bedroom house for them, her brother and sister and then her and a baby too? She couldn't imagine it. And what about their religious values? One thing was certain she could not imagine they'd say she should have an abortion, an unheard of possibility at that time. No, she and Peter would have had to get married changing her whole life drastically. Mother Elias wondered, "Better? Worse? Who's to say? Who's to know? There's no point wondering all these years later what might have been if..."

She looked deeply again into the eyes of the young nun sitting beside her remembering suddenly what one of her students at a girls' boarding school many years ago announced to her one day, "You should have been a Mother." At the time she just more or less laughed off the comment, but today approaching seventy, it came back to her in a wave of nostalgia for what she would never be, at least not biologically. A memory flashed across her mind. She was only nineteen and in the convent only about a year. She was assigned to help out at the nun's old age home in the country. Every morning one poor old nun would stand at her cell or bedroom door crying for her son. Was he real or only a figment of her deluded mind? No one ever knew.

She really considered Mary of all the other nuns in her care as the daughter she would never have. She loved her deeply and wanted to do whatever she could to make her happy. Besides the Community really needed the money her Father planned to donate. They couldn't afford to lose that.

"Sister Mary, my sense is that for at least the time being, we keep the status quo. You do all you can to be a good nun and I will support you on whatever you decide about your future."

"Thank you so much, Mother Elias. May I leave now?"

"Yes, but please promise me that you'll talk to me any time you feel the need."

To herself the Superior added, "Oh, how I sincerely hope you will do that, my dear." Then as the young nun left her office,

Mother Elias sighed deeply, but Sister Mary would never know why. Since she first met her, she'd been questioning her own vocation even though she would celebrate her Golden Jubilee of fifty years in the convent in only five years. Could she actually leave this special way of life after all these years? How would she survive? Who would hire her in her mid-sixties? She had only one choice - to remain a religious and be the best surrogate Mother she could be to each of the young nuns especially the poor sad one who had just left her office.

She sat staring out the window of her office for a long time. She should do something more to help Sister Mary who as far as she could tell was suffering from postpartum depression. And no wonder without a husband or even just a male friend to support her and no baby to hold. She had to do something to get her beyond this down time. Picking up her phone, she dialed the number of a priest friend to whom she had referred several of the young nuns in her charge who were also suffering emotional traumas.

A week later again with Sister Ramona as her companion, Sister Mary dutifully rode the local bus to Father William's rectory. How she survived that afternoon was another of the main mysteries of her life. Being urged to go into another room off the man's office. Only realizing then what he intended to do. It was like an upside down version of her time on the boat with James. But now... but now... she was repulsed knowing that this stranger, this supposed "Man of God" actually intended to... so she'd feel better! Swaying back and forth with pain in her gut, she remembered a punch she levied in his... area... then his roaring scream and curse, "Jesus Christ! You disgusting little witch!"

It was as though her own Father had become this man and she had punched him in his privates. On some strange level she felt better already as she propelled her way out of the room to the one where her companion waited for her. She never told anyone, not even Mother Elias, what had almost happened that day when she resolved no man would ever touch her body again.

When she finally fell asleep that night, another nightmare assaulted her.

In a karate class on the verge of becoming a Black Belt, the naked instructor grabbed her and threw her on the floor holding her down with a very long living zipper that laughed crazily at her. Before she could get her wits about her, she became a sniveling little girl literally crying her eyes out for her Mommy. She, of course, couldn't see the instructor grab her by her throat. Then he yelped, "There's no getting away from me this time, you loathsome substitute for a woman of God!"

When Mary managed to jerk awake, she realized her long white nightgown and sheet were completely soaked. Apparently, she had lost control of herself during the trauma of the nightmare. She had read some books and articles on dreams so she more or less understood what her unconscious was trying to tell her: She was reliving the daymare with Father William, but no matter what the events of the nightmare were, in real life she had been anything but a sniveling little girl. She had stood her ground and did get away from the disgusting substitute of a holy priest. Throughout the rest of her life, when she felt pushed to the wall, she'd remember this dream and oddly be reassured she could survive whatever confronted her, even if it were a very long living zipper of all things!

Sister Eustacia looked around her transfixed by what she saw now and where she was out of the blue... on a boat with wild teenage sounds! Not music like an orchestra would play. On the water surrounded by huge container ships. Many floored condos mostly unoccupied she guessed. Tall steel structures that looked like gigantic insects from outer space. Sail boats floating by. Motor boats zipping by... zip... zipper... Should have kept it up... why, how, where was she?

As Sister Mary walked down the hall when she returned to the Motherhouse after her unusual rejuvenating experience with Father William, she thought about how soon her forced stay behind these walls would be over. She had been brought here last September. Left for the Home in October. Returned to the Motherhouse in April. Now she only had four more months left to decide whether she'd stay a nun for the rest of her life or leave the convent for good.

Mysteriously, the words from the opening of the Mass many years before sneaked back into her ears, "I will go to the altar of God, to God, the Joy of my Youth." Had He really been her Joy through all her decades of submission to her superiors, of denial of her femininity, of penance for her sins? Had He been her Joy through all of that? No, He had left her on her own during most of those years in her soul's private Dark Night. Bereft without her daughter. Not knowing for sure what happened to her little one or to James. Hurting inside so much that tears gushed from her eyes without warning sometime without apparent provocation.

Even when she was teaching high school English, a line from a poem or a scene from a novel would make her so sad she couldn't contain herself. One day in particular she remembered reading a Christina Rossetti poem called "A Daughter of Eve" to her class. As the final lines, "Stripped bare of hope and everything// No more to laugh, no more to sing// I sit alone in sorrow" flowed out of her mouth, she all but collapsed on the floor and ran out of the room suddenly as she grieved for her baby. She still wanted to believe she was alive and well after all these years. Her baby girl she never even got to hold in her arms. Her baby girl the nurse told her died. Her baby girl she heard others say was given away. "I sit alone in sorrow. No more to laugh or sing."

"No, no, they couldn't have done that!" she bellowed.

Her aide came to her side immediately as she continued to moan, "Please, God, no!"

"Is there anything I can do for you, Sister?" Julie asked quietly.

The befuddled old lady could only peer at the young woman and beg her, "Oh please, oh please find my baby girl and James too!"

The young girl rolled her eyes she thought for the twentieth time this afternoon. Squeezing Sister's liver pocked hand, she urged, "Here let me help you to the ladies' room, Sister. Maybe you'll feel better after you wash your face."

"No! I don't need to do that. I need to find them. Do you know where they are? Can you help me find them?" Then she bellowed again, "Please, for the love of God please help me. I can't go on without my little one and my James!"

From her disjointed memory Mary, inexplicably again Sister Eustacia, couldn't recall why James had been so important in her life. She didn't know what love was. Her Father was too strict and severe. Yes, her Mother spoiled her as an only child but how was that really love? Neither one ever showed her any real affection, never hugged her or kissed her scrapes when she fell. She could hear her Father always chiding her instead, "Why didn't you pay attention where you were walking? You should have known better!" Never saying, "Here let me kiss it and make it all right."

Certainly sexual love for a man wasn't an experience she understood. She couldn't remember why she would have loved this James of her vague memory. Did she know him a long time? Had he said he really cared about her? Did they go out on real dates? Did he stay by her when she really needed him? Could he have stood up to her Father if he had to for her sake?

Flashes of scenes of her life whisked across her mind. An extremely handsome man smiling at her. Then tickling her. Being so close to her she could feel his heart. Seeing him take money from her Father. Then gone forever from her life after that. A baby kicking in her stomach. Then she too Gone! Gone! Gone!

How could she say she loved this man? This elusive James from somewhere in her twisted memory. Where was he when their child was born if he loved her as she loved him? Did she really love him? How could she have? What was happening to her? She couldn't decide what was real in her memory or what wasn't. Who could she depend on? What could she believe? She didn't know. Actually, she couldn't know. Her mind was a demented magician playing bizarre tricks on her. She just didn't realize it.

Who was this man named James anyway? She'd heard herself call out his name at odd times but didn't know why. Then small rooms called cabins peered at her out of the ocean of her memories. She saw a very young girl with an extremely short haircut running crazily up a narrow staircase behind a tall man at least a few years older than her laughing almost hysterically all the way up three flights. Her knees shone bright red. Then the two tumbled into a bed without clothes on. It didn't make any sense. Who was this James? Was she with him in this small room called a cabin? Why?

Her head ached violently now from trying so hard to put all the pieces of the puzzles of her memory together. In her mind she asked, "James, who were you? Who are you? Where are you? Why do I keep saying your name?"

Sister's mind was caught in a quicksand of queries, none of them with any answers. She slumped lower in her chair and looked out over the water. Was it the Atlantic Ocean or maybe the Baltimore Harbor? For the life of her, she couldn't decide which. Her body shook wildly as her aide pushed her wheelchair. On the way across the room, she noticed the wrinkled waitress who had served her lunch smile at her.

She was reminded of a visitor last week. A really old man with a head of pure white hair walking with a cane... old enough to have been her James' Grandfather. Got rid of him before...

Somewhere in the dark of the back of her mind, she remembered that there was something about the old man's eyes.

Sister continued to be caught in a circle about the evening of the greatest fun of her life followed quickly by the lowest level too! She would never have any way of knowing that when James took her Father's bribe not to see her again, he donated it to a local children's hospital where he was working as an aide at the time. Years later he did his residency there and stayed on as a full-time pediatrician. He lost touch with Mary when her Father made her enter the convent. After many searches over the years, when he finally tracked her down after he retired, he realized in his still lucid mind that she in her confused mind expected a tall young man with curly black hair, not some old white-haired guy leaning on a cane. There was nothing for him to do but leave when she yelled for him to get out of her room. What regrets he had that he didn't find her before...

When the old nun and her young aide returned to the table, everyone was stirring on the harbor cruise getting ready to disembark. For Sister Eustacia that meant returning to Saint Clara's Retirement Home where she'd been living since she was eighty. At least there she didn't have to do chores any more like serve meals, clean all the rooms, polish furniture and floors, fine stitch the yards upon yards of the hem of her floor-length habit, cut up pounds upon pounds of carrots or potatoes or fruit for the nuns like she did in those early years in the Community.

The Community. What it had meant to her over the years like when the Stock Market crashed and she got the news that her Father had lost everything. Then weeks later the tragic follow up news that he had jumped out of his eighteenth floor office. She'd been so wiped out with pneumonia then that the doctor wouldn't let her attend his funeral, not that she had any energy or desire to go against his wishes except if she could have for her dear Mother's sake.

Then unbelievably months later, she received another message that nearly sent her over the edge herself. Her Mother was very ill with a disease that had ravaged her body leaving her with only months to live. There was nothing the doctors could do to save her. Sister Eustacia was permitted to visit her in the hospital only once before she died. It helped her so much that Mother Elias was her companion.

When Mary walked into her Mother's hospital room, the hospital chaplain was giving her the Last Rites. The woman she once loved was just a shell of a human being. When her eyes fluttered open, she smiled wanly at her daughter.

"Hello, Mother. I'm so happy to see you," Mary lied as she felt nauseous.

"Yes, Mary... my darling... I... I...," she responded. She was obviously in pain having trouble talking. "Mary... my dear... I have to... tell you... I'm so sorry about what... your Father...."

"It's OK, Mother. Please don't worry about him anymore."

Sister would never forget her Mother's final words to her a short time later, "I'm so... sorry... for... every... thing... dear Mary... stay... a... good... nun... I... love... you."

"I love you, Mother. I will do as you wish."

Mother Elias took the young nun's shaking body in her

arms and held it for a long time. Then Sister reached up and closed her Mother's eyes as Mother Elias summoned the nurse. They left the hospital hand in hand. Looking back, Mary knew she wouldn't have survived that ordeal if Mother Elias hadn't been there with her.

Because of the specifics of the Rule at the time, Mary could only attend her Mother's funeral with a Sister companion, again fortunately Mother Elias. But she wasn't permitted to go to the cemetery afterwards. Over the years she tried to assure herself it was for the best saving her additional heartbreak, but she was never completely convinced.

Through those grievous times her sisters, especially Mother Elias, rallied round her trying to ease her suffering. Each in her own way attempted to commiserate, counsel and console her but were successful only to a certain degree. It was always her surrogate Mother, Mother Elias, who went out of her way to be extra understanding and even give her special privileges like being able to take a walk by herself or sleep in past dawn once in a while. And so her fate was set. She would remain a nun and strive with all her heart to be a good one as her dying biological Mother had asked her.

She could almost feel herself the morning of her Final Profession, what some people thought of as her marriage to God. She wore a crown of red roses on her head and a floor length white veil that Mother Elias replaced by the altar with a black one. During the prostration when she and the other eight women she entered with lay stomach down on the altar floor, covered by a long black pall to symbolize their death to "the world, the flesh and the devil," she heard herself say to James, "Good bye. We weren't meant to be together. I am all God's from today on with my three vows of poverty, chastity and obedience." She could also hear in her mind the sisters' choir singing, "Forever thine, my Jesus. Forever."

"Yes, Jesus loves me. Yes, Jesus loves me. The Bible tells me so," lines of a song her best friend from childhood used to sing from her Bible class, flowed into in her mind and then on her lips softly at first then louder and louder. Now even other guests on the other side of the boat turned in her direction. Then apparently embarrassed for her, turned away again quickly.

"Sister, Sister," her aide interrupted, "would you like a little spin around the room to see the sights we're passing?"

"That sounds like a fine idea. Maybe I'll see James along the way somewhere," Sister answered excitedly.

Julie shook her head again as she became like an impromptu travel guide for the old nun as she pointed the tall ship container cranes, Fort McHenry, Fells Point, Federal Hill, the USS Constitution, and the John W. Brown Liberty Ship. Sister ooohed and ahhhed as she was wheeled around. Suddenly, she stopped the wheelchair and asked the young girl, "But where are the huge ocean waves I saw yesterday? I don't see any out there anymore."

"That's because this isn't the ocean, Sister. It's the Baltimore Harbor."

"But I don't understand Father and Mother and I are on our way to Paris. Don't we have to cross the Atlantic Ocean to get there?"

"Well, yes, you would, Sister, but...."

"So what are you trying to tell me? Are we on the Ile de France on our way to Paris or not?" Sister's voice had risen several decibels in the past few minutes. Her aide's face was reddening in concert with it. Fortunately for her, one of Sister's closest friends, Sister Joseph, realized the young girl's distress and came to her rescue.

"Thank you so much for wheeling Sister around, Julie. I'll take over now."

Relieved, the aide scurried up the stairs to the top deck to clear her mind. She felt so sorry for Sister Eustacia and so incapable of helping her. Ah, but the cool breeze outside really calmed her.

As her friend continued to push her around the room, Sister remembered the day she was given her name in religion "Eustacia" meaning "The Tranquil One" despite the fact that it was apparently based on "Eustadiola," a matron of a French noble family in Bourges 1,400 years ago. After the death of her husband, this holy woman founded a convent and built many churches. Mary felt the variation on her name suited her well thinking about the wealthy family she grew up in and especially about how she lost her James. How he had effectively died to her. Oh, how she still missed him!

There were many days she rued the fact that she had honored her Mother's dying wish to "stay a good nun." Some nights she hugged herself to sleep wishing she could be somewhere else, like in the arms of a man like James who would love her just as she was, for whatever she was. She longed for that solace denied her by her vow of chastity. Some days she felt so bereft she thought she would die.

Out of her disjointed memory came flashes of scenes. Trying to learn to use a treadle sewing machine. Being required to eat whatever was served at meals. Especially abhorring hot raisins for breakfast. Not considering a baked half grapefruit dessert every Sunday at lunch. Being fooled by a friend who would tie the back pieces of her veil together before she walked out on the main altar to clean. Laughing about crazy things like how her lips trembled every time she corrected one of her seventh graders the first year she taught. Hearing a student ask her, "When are you going to leave?" the first year she taught at a boarding school. Maybe she should have then but... her Mother said she should stay a good nun so she did. Special parties at Christmas and other holidays when sometimes they could drink a glass of wine. The surprise of square dancing two nights after entering when she had thought ahead of time she would never dance again. Having lots of fun though with all women many laughs keeping straight which sisters were to be the men. Ahh and swimming in the college pool so much fun but so weird having to keep silence in the water and in the dressing room. Always thinking it was so strange they could only talk in a doorway in an emergency after the Grand Silence at 9 pm. Being required to do something like sew instead of just talking at recreation from 8 to 9 at night. Eating the one piece of chocolate passed out then except during Advent and Lent. Having to have a companion to go to the dentist or doctor or wherever....

It was now nearly eight decades since the day she first walked into the hallowed halls of the Motherhouse and became one of the "Good Sisters," a description that always incensed her since she was well aware that not all of the "holy" nuns were, in fact, that "holy" at all, not to mention some priests like the one who had tried to violate her. She recalled hearing years after the fact about a nun she once taught with who had an affair with a workman at the convent. Another who was sent home for being a lesbian though no one ever actually said that word then. Or another who was told by a lecherous "holy" priest that the way to remedy her depression was to go to bed with him which she did and suffered a nervous breakdown as a result. Mary knew her guardian angel was really with her the day the same thing didn't actually happen to her.

Of course, Mother Elias was a major exception to these people. She treated Sister Mary and the other young nuns in her care with respect and kindness. Thinking back over all those years, Mary knew she would never have survived without her support. She might have killed herself otherwise or, worse, her Father might have done the deed if he ever found out about her pregnancy and the subsequent birth of her stillborn daughter. Yes, without a doubt Mother Elias made all the difference in her life. Mary really didn't even want to imagine what would have happened to her if....

She hated remembering those ordinary unholy nuns of every day who thrived on cutting down their fellow sisters, telling exaggerated stories about them that were sometimes outright lies, refusing to talk to certain sisters because they had inadvertently hurt them in some way, or simply being mean or rude to their fellow sisters no matter what the reason.

It was those every day ordinary unholy ones who had hurt Sister Eustacia the most during her years behind convent walls. They cut her down because she wasn't kneeling in chapel for as long as they were or not lounging with them in the community room watching Perry Mason, the only TV show they were allowed to see when restrictions against watching television were lifted. All the while she'd be out volunteering her free time visiting the sick nuns in the infirmary or teaching a religion class for the public school kids or being a server for Sunday Mass at the local juvenile detention home. These "holy" nuns falsely judged her for whatever she did or didn't do. These unholy ones always found ways to try to dishonor her or belittle her. But never to her face! No, it was almost always behind her back. She'd only hear about what they were saying from a sister friend or sometimes overhear a conversation not intended for her ears. Or was it?

The saddest thing was she couldn't run to Mother Elias to talk about the wrongs they did to her. As a Professed nun she lived in a local house many miles away from the Motherhouse where Mother Elias continued to take care of the new nuns. How Mary missed her! She wished she could talk to her again whenever she felt the need. But no, now she had to face all the problems on her own. Aside from some close friends in the ranks with her, there was no other superior she really trusted. What a sad reality that was for her.

With a smile she recalled some of the good times too behind those hallowed walls. Out of the blue of the day on the luncheon cruise as everyone was getting ready to leave, she was a young novice again enjoying square dancing, putting on special holiday skits for the Community and sharing crazy stories of what happened in her classroom with her fellow nuns over dinner. Sister remembered her close friends for life from those days, several were sitting at the table on the cruise with her, but she couldn't figure out how at the same time they could be here and there on the Ile de France celebrating her sixteenth birthday. Why weren't they dressed up like she was? Why didn't they have their hair bobbed and their knees painted red? Where was the champagne her Father and later James had given her? She loved the sparkling taste of it going down her throat. Oh and what happened to her birthday cake? Did everyone eat it already? She couldn't remember enjoying even one little piece of it....

Again inexplicably, she found herself back in the early days of her life in the convent when she had enjoyed some good times with a few nuns who became her close friends. Their friendship, the quiet and, of course, her college education certainly helped her a lot so on some level she really didn't regret staying for all these eight decades, but still... somewhere James was waiting for her with their little daughter who was crying for her Momma. Could she have found both of them if she had tried harder? Wanted it to happen more? Would there have been a way she never thought of? Was there some other ways she never thought about that she might have found them? If she had begged her Father with all his money, couldn't he have found them for her? But no, he would never have even listened to her, let alone gone overboard to help her. No, James and their little one were lost to her forever!

It hit her then what she could or should or might have done. It was an overwhelming thought at first, but as she pondered it, it made more and more sense. She should have left the convent after her Father committed suicide because she shouldn't have been afraid of him anymore. So why did she stay? If she had been on the other side of those walls, she would have been able to search for James and their little one in ways she couldn't have in the convent. Her regret was a huge hard pill to swallow. Some days she almost couldn't get it down.

The problem was she had promised her dying Mother that she would "stay a good nun." So she determined she would be just that over the years. Though there were good times, they were mostly wiped out by the unfair and untrue criticisms of her being bandied about behind her back her by the unholy ones, the mean and hateful ones, the jealous ones. In the naiveté of her earliest days there, she couldn't understand how women who had dedicated their lives to God could have the same weaknesses and sinful behaviors of those on the outside. It still shocked her sometimes that some of them harbored resentment and anger and jealousy toward her. Even today?

No, not today. Today she was just sixteen having the time of her life on a gigantic ship called the Ile de France with her very wealthy Father and her loving and caring Mother.

How could any of those less than holy nuns be here? She didn't even know any. She had no connections to any. She had no understanding of their life style or the way they dressed or anything when she was sixteen.

To give back to others what she had been given, she had

worked very hard at a mission for "unweds" like she had been and felt great joy when their babies were born and flourished. Through those years she continued to wonder about her own daughter. Could she still possibly be alive somewhere? If so, did she have a happy childhood with whatever family took her in? Did she marry and have her own children? Or was she really dead? Had she really been stillborn as she had been told so many years ago? She doubted that she'd ever know for sure, but how she yearned with her whole heart and soul for that knowledge. How many times had her poor body ached to hold her baby daughter in her arms, to have her quietly nursing, to love and cherish and raise her into a fine woman. But God or Fate or whoever had other plans for her.

Sister vaguely remembered teaching many, many teenagers, thousands of them over the course of the forty years she spent in the classroom. She knew she should still be out there in some school helping them now, but she realized at least on odd occasions that she forgot so many things so often, had difficulty remembering where she was at times and just couldn't connect all the dots of her life anymore. As a result she was put "out to pasture" by her Superiors as she came to think of her life at Saint Clara's Retirement Home. Although it was a nice place, she missed Mother Elias who was always so kind to her until... that horrible day when... heart attack... put in the ground... in Heaven with her Mother now... maybe James and their little baby daughter too. Oh, where could she go to find them? Why did all of them have to leave her? Oh! Oh! Why?

Her parents always gave her everything she wanted like a new and more lovely doll to replace one she lost. Even her own special white pony she named "Ivory" but no, they couldn't get her James or their baby daughter back to her. Oh, no! Oh no!

Through her tears, Sister felt her wheelchair being pulled away from the table. The same nice young men who earlier reminded her of James, the young man with the sparkling blue-green eyes she met just yesterday on the big boat to Paris, were helping her aide maneuver the wheelchair down the runway to the sidewalk.

Sister turned as they moved her, noticing the wrinkle-faced waitress from the boat watching them from the window. For some reason she couldn't comprehend, she wished she had said goodbye to her.

PART II

NAOMI
Holding On

"I'll find you in the morning sun
And when the night is new
I'll be looking at the moon
But I'll be seeing you."

(Kahal/Fain 1944)

Chapter 4

A Daughter's Death

Naomi stood at the window for a long time watching the elderly nuns leave the boat and thinking about the easy lives they have. No worries about children or grandchildren like she always had. No worries about money. No worries about how they'd be cared for in their Golden Years. Those nuns were so damn lucky! Having everything just given to them free and effortless. Nice houses. Good food and clothes. Most of all, each other for support and companionship.

What did they know about real problems like the ones she'd been facing every day of her frigging life? Especially that one with the crooked headpiece who was celebrating her ninety-fifth birthday on the luncheon cruise ship today. Naomi doubted that she'd ever make it to that age. She always felt so tired and in pain from the arthritis in her legs and hands, but her twin grandsons Ted and Tom needed her so much. In their mid-twenties and in graduate school, Naomi knew that whatever she could do for them, their Mother, her only child, her Lovely Lily, her Flower, would have wanted her to do. No matter what. No matter how. No matter how tired she was to the ends of her entire being as she always was! On her feet all day running back and forth, back and forth bowing and scraping to nearly every person on the cruise. Even getting the damn extra candles for that old nun's birthday cake. That's when she knew for sure that she was increasingly spaced out. Imagine insisting there be sixteen candles on the cake! How crazy was that? What world was she living in?

Naomi could only imagine a typical day that old nun and her fellow sisters might have in their perfect world at Saint Clara's Retirement Home. Naturally every morning a healthy breakfast would be cooked and served to them. Then maybe they'd pray for an hour or so and after that read or sew or do whatever else with no one bothering them. After lunch, also cooked and served to them, they'd take a walk or a nap or maybe go to the library on site. Then dinner would be cooked and served to them and they'd probably say a few more prayers and later sit around and talk to each other. They'd have no worries about jobs or insurance or groceries or kids or grandkids or husbands or parents or health care or laundry or money or anything! How lucky could they be? They sure as hell all lived a real Life of Riley! There was no denying that.

Never in her whole life had she had it as easy as those old nuns do every day! She always had to work for every scrap of food for her table. For every single almighty dollar in her pocket! Slaving at a pitiful seven dollars an hour job she almost had to beg the owner on her knees to get! She forced herself to continue working way after she turned sixty-five despite all her aches and pains, some of which went way beyond being simply physical ones. They subsided more or less with meds or time, but her deep emotional problems hung on and on and some even haunted her like ones flowing in and out of her memory about her Lovely Lily, her Flower.

Would she ever be able to rest? Really rest like that nun with her headpiece on crooked could every day and night in her fancy retirement home? No, she couldn't see how that could ever happen to her. She hadn't been blessed like that old nun or any of her sisters. They all had it made and then some!

Her life started to go down the toilet right when she ended up at Saint Justin's Orphanage. Naomi always wondered why fate took away her Mother and Father? In her mind's eye she could picture herself as a tiny newborn crying for her Mother, being held by a stranger and then raised by a series of other strangers, some of them mean and hateful, others only taking her in for the money and barely acknowledging her existence. She was in their homes to help them not the other way around.

And who was her Father? She'd never know him just like her Lovely Lily, her Flower would never know for sure who fathered her twin sons. But that was her fault. Naomi had no choice in the matter. "What a crock of crap Fate has thrown in my face!" she complained to herself.

Childhood had never really happened for her at all. Following the Orphanage, which she didn't really remember, she was sent to one dysfunctional foster home after another. Each one seemed worse than the one before. She didn't even want to think about these so-called foster homes, how many or where they were for they were all horrible. But not as bad as....

Oh, how she regretted letting the memory of her adoptive parents surface in her mind! All the pain, both physical and emotional, they caused her. Even after all these years, she felt physically sick remembering how much they hurt her in so many ways she wished she could forget. Of course, she knew there was no way to do that. The bad memories of all those years had a way of surfacing at odd times, usually disturbingly.

Like now as she watched that nun being helped out in her wheelchair. For some unknown reason that made her remember a nightmare she had decades ago which had plagued her ever since...

She was being forced to work in a coal mine miles underground by an evil mad woman. She coughed and nearly choked and fell over from lack of air, but she had to go on. She had to keep on working. She needed every cent she could lay her hands on to take home to her false family even if that meant agreeing to stay in this wretched place forever! All of a sudden she heard the mad woman scream out her name. Oh no, she knew that meant she'd have to go deeper and deeper down in the pit! Maybe she'd never be able to crawl her way back up and out ever again....

How she hated it every time that nightmare regurgitated in her memory like the taste of a sip of sour milk! What she really needed right now was a freaking cigarette, but like so often these days, she didn't have even one in her purse. Oh, but that cute Suzy, the newest young thing waitress, was always nice enough to give her a few. She stumbled down the stairs of the boat to find her.

Later as she sat puffing away, she recalled how hard she tried years ago to come to terms with never having a real Mother. "Fate took her away from me but maybe she is watching me from above," she imagined, "protecting and guiding me throughout my life."

But her cynical self argued, "Well, she can't be watching over me otherwise she would never let those despicable adoptive parents enslave me. If she wouldn't help me when I was a helpless little child, then why should I even consider that she'd help me now? She probably wouldn't even want to waste her time with me now that I'm so damn old. But why did she have to leave me so alone in this world?"

Her good self countered, "But how do you know she has not been helping you? Maybe your Mother in Heaven is doing all she can and you would have been worse off otherwise."

"If she was helping you at all while living with all those foster families who took advantage of you and then with those abusive adoptive parents, then you don't need her kind of help. Sure, you were better off with them, not your own Mother!" her cynical self replied passionately.

"No! No! No!" her good self responded, "You don't know what would have happened otherwise. Maybe she thought you'd have a chance at a better life away from her."

Stopping this inner debate at that point, Naomi mumbled, "What's past is past," knowing she could say the words but didn't really believe them. Knew she couldn't live them. Knew she might as well be stuck working in the coal mine of her recurrent nightmare forever. That's how much Old Man Fate had done her in, by damn! He really hated her!

How she wished she could go back and have another crack at all that had happened to her over the years, changing all the bad stuff so she could get all the good things she had missed.

She could hope, couldn't she? She'd been doing that all her pitiful life but always losing the game she called "Looking

Out for a Better Tomorrow." Certainly, she could look for it, yearn for it and search for it endlessly, even though it most likely wasn't anywhere on the horizon waiting for her. No, she might as well just give up on that hope already. How long could she go on hoping for the impossible?

"Naomi, ready to go?" It was Smithy, her ride, calling her. He worked maintenance on the boat and lived in her apartment building. She grabbed her worn out purse she bought at a local thrift store and trudged back up the stairs and down the runway to meet him finally in the lot across the street from the boat. He was a godsend since she couldn't afford a car and riding a crowded bus always sapped the little strength she had left over at the end of a day on the boat. She had to keep some energy to take care of her grandsons.

For she knew all too well what was waiting for her at home. Laundry, multiple loads. A sink full of dirty dishes. Beds to be made. Dinner to cook. The apartment to straighten up. Her grandsons would be home tonight by six so she'd have to get moving. Oh, she never got any real rest always going from one job to another and another.

She trudged up the three flights to the apartment she shared with her "two boys," as she always called her twin grandsons. Over twenty years ago her only daughter, her Lovely Lily, her Flower, had nearly died giving birth to them within nine minutes of each other. Of course, her bad habits didn't help the situation. All her drinking and carousing. She did cut back a bit several months before her babies were born, but like a snake slithering back to bite her, she got hers in the end. How absolutely dreadful that was!

Naomi had found her body right inside the door of their apartment building one morning when Ted and Tom were only nine. Her Lovely Lily, her Flower, had apparently come home from her favorite bar so drunk she lost her footing, hit her head on the edge of the old radiator in the hall and bled to death during the early morning hours. Fortunately, Naomi found her on her way to work at a local department store instead of her grandsons on their way to school. That would have been so much more traumatic for the two of them as kids to see their Mother lifeless like that!

In the panic of the moment, Naomi pounded on the nearest apartment door and yelled at the old lady who answered to call 911.

While waiting for the ambulance, she sat on the floor holding the cold body of her Lovely Lily, her Flower in her arms as she talked to her as though she were still alive. "Oh my dearest daughter, I am so sorry I haven't been a very good Mother. I apologize for my mistakes, my weaknesses, my poor attempts to get you help and lead you away form all the bad influences of your young life that had to end like this. All I can do now to make up for everything is to be the best substitute Mother to your boys."

In her mind's ear she heard her Lovely Lily, her Flower answer her, "Oh, Mom, I was always my own best enemy. I know how much you tried to steer me away from all the temptations I gave into so easily."

Naomi was so distraught she readily answered her out loud, "Lily, Lily, my Flower, how I've always loved you! You brought me so much joy especially when I thought my life was over. I'm so sorry I couldn't have reached you before...."

Lily's voice interrupted, "Mom, please don't do this to yourself. I'm the one to blame. I ignored your attempts to help me. I was determined to go my own direction. It wasn't your fault I ended up this way."

Through her raging tears, Naomi hugged her broken daughter's body one last time as the scream of the ambulance rang through the street. When the paramedics entered the building, she heard Lily's final words. "I'm so sorry. I've always loved you. You did all you could for me and more. Thank you. Thank you. Thank you." Those words echoed in her head as the paramedics had to pull Lily out of Naomi's embrace.

She shivered remembering the horrors of the days after her Lovely Lily, her Flower died which kept coming back to her in a trio of recurrent nightmares almost every night.

In one she was trying to drag the comatose body of a young woman out of a hell hole, but it wouldn't budge no matter how hard she pulled and pulled. All of a sudden it looked her right in the face, spit at her and then screamed, "Why didn't you come to save me, you horrible excuse of a Mother?" Sewn shut, Naomi's mouth just twitched noiselessly.

In another she was watching as a drunken woman nearly fell out of a bar into a cab, but the surly driver, disgusted by her condition, pushed her roughly back out on the sidewalk and zoomed away leaving her there where she choked on her own vomit. Naomi saw herself standing nearby just staring at the woman's body as it lay motionless. She was cemented to the sidewalk. All she could do was scream soundlessly.

In the third and most disturbing one of all, she was one of her grandsons bounding down the stairs of the apartment in a happy hurry to get to school when he tripped over the body of someone. As he slid on the puddle of blood, he fell right beside the woman's ashen face, the face of his Mommy!

For more nights than Naomi could recall, all three of these recurrent nightmares assailed her one after the other the whole night. It was no wonder she hardly ever got a good night's sleep. Her unresolved guilt was like an Avenging Angel trying to suck out her very soul. Try as she might, sleep brought her no respite from her pain. She suffered through her Lovely Lily, her Flower's death over and over again, totally helpless to save her each time.

How well she remembered every word of the conversation she had with Maya, the bartender at her Lovely Lily, her Flower's favorite pub, several days after she died. Maya had come by her apartment to offer her condolences. The two of them ended up sharing much more than they initially intended.

"Oh how sorry I was to hear about your daughter's passing, Naomi!" Maya said as soon as Naomi opened the door of her apartment. She tried to put her arms around her in empathy, but Naomi recoiled from her attempt.

"Is that so, Maya? She got drunk again that night at your bar, didn't she?"

"Yes, unfortunately, she did but...."

"Remember how I begged you so many times almost on my knees not to keep serving her but you...."

"Oh, Naomi, I...."

"You what? Just needed the money for your daughter's college tuition so you didn't care what happened to my Lovely Lily, my Flower? That's right, isn't it?" Naomi's voice rose to a scream startling Maya.

"No, Naomi, that's not true and you know it! I really tried my best to keep her from drinking so much or too much. Oh, how I tried!" Maya held back the tears now surging to the edges of her eyes. She was embarrassed to let Naomi know how upset and how guilty she actually felt.

Naomi was on the verge of losing it too. She knew no

matter how much blame she tried to pin on Maya, it was more her own fault that her Lovely Lily, her Flower had died when she did and the way she did. No one could convince her otherwise.

"Maya, please listen to me. I know you really tried to save my Lovely Lily, my Flower from herself and her worst enemy, the bottle. The only thing I wonder is why you didn't call me that night to pick her up like you'd done many other times."

"I've thought a lot about how I'd answer that question which I knew you'd ask me some day, Naomi. My bouncer Jake fell sick with the flu and suddenly left that night and I couldn't find a replacement. He usually helps people who need to get home safely and would've helped Lily as he'd done a number of times before. But I got so busy with a rowdy bachelor party creating trouble that I forgot Jake wasn't there. By the time I remembered Lily was already gone. It was only today, three days later, that I heard what happened to her. Oh, Naomi, I'm so sorry for what happened!"

"Oh, I know you have to feel this way, Maya, but my Lovely Lily, my Flower was a grown woman though an extremely immature one as you well knew. She had a mind of her own which I couldn't change, so how could you who hardly knew her do it? It was mostly because of my own damn failings that she turned out so rotten! True, you probably helped her along, but even if you hadn't given her any more booze, she'd have found another place and another bartender or have gone to some store to buy some whiskey or beer herself. I've done a lot of hard thinking lately and know for a fact that I am mostly to blame for my Lovely Lily, my Flower's death."

Naomi wondered for a moment why her Lovely Lily Her Flower had turned out the way she did. Where had she gone wrong as her Mother and Father combined? Didn't she love her enough? Guide her in the right directions? Teach her better? Or did she go off the deep end because she never had a Father or even a Father figure in her life? Never had a man's strength, his shoulder to cry on, his good influence. Oh why, why did her Lovely Lily Her Flower end up going off with the wrong crowd? The wrong guys? Why couldn't she have listened to all Naomi tired to teach her from her earliest days? Why?

Returning to the situation, Naomi continued, "I never could reach her and never was able to keep her away from the bad apples she associated with. There was this one guy everyone called Buddy. He was such a jerk he wouldn't even take her on a regular date like maybe to dinner and a movie. No, all they did together was go bar hopping drinking lots of money away. Mostly mine I had given her for bus fare or clothes. I couldn't convince her to stop all the bad things she was doing no matter how hard I tried. I've been the all-time worst Mother! Now I'm trying to make up for that by taking extra good care of my two grandsons."

"It sounds like both of us have a lot of forgiving of

ourselves to do, Naomi." At that Maya stretched out her arms and pulled Naomi into a big hug. This time she didn't recoil from her embrace so the two women cried for many minutes in each other's arms. When their tears dried up, they squeezed each other's hands realizing instinctively that their mutual guilt about Lily's demise would keep them friends.

What Naomi didn't admit to Maya or to anyone else for that matter was that sometimes during the day she thought she saw her Lovely Lily, her Flower traipsing along the sidewalk or almost falling into the Baltimore harbor by the luncheon cruise ship. How many times she had stopped abruptly to make sure it wasn't her. One time she even tried to hug an unsuspecting young woman thinking she was her Lovely Lily, her Flower, but then the woman screamed and Naomi dropped her arms as though they were on fire. After that woman fled down the street, Naomi sat down on the bench nearby and stared out across the harbor for a long time in pain.

Of late she believed she was starting to get like that old nun who was celebrating her ninety-fifth birthday on the boat. Out of touch with reality. Hoping against hope to change the past somehow. To wipe away all her guilt, depression and remorse. Would she even make it anyway near her mid-nineties at the rate she was going? She seriously doubted it. She wasn't cared for like those old nuns in their last years. No, she had to fend for herself all the time. She had no other choice thanks to Old Man

Fate!

One thing she really felt good about though. She had worked very hard over the years to shield her grandsons from the ghastly facts about their Mother's death. Not telling them all the gory details and just saying she fell and hit her head. After all they were only babies in a way at the time of the tragedy. Only nine years old.

But then came the terrible day when they were twelve and both limped in the door of the apartment home from school late, their bodies bruised and bloody. From what she could get out of them, several bullies had ganged up on them calling their Mother "a no good drunk" so they had fought to try to convince them they were wrong. The worst part for Naomi was after she cleaned and bandaged her grandsons' wounds, they peered into her eyes, all innocence gone from them, and asked, "It's true, isn't it, Grandma?"

Naomi only had the courage to hug them both close to herself and answer softly, "Yes, my dear ones, it is."

Later when they scrambled off to their rooms to do their homework, Naomi recalled a conversation they had with her when they were only six years old while their Mother was sleeping off a night on the town upstairs.

Tom began, "Grandma, we know we have a Mommy and you to take care of us, but where's our Daddy? Our friend Larry said everyone has both somewhere even if they don't live in the same house."

Naomi gritted her teeth knowing they'd surely ask this question someday. She hoped she'd say the right words to satisfy them, "Your friend is right, Honey, you had a Daddy, but your Mommy doesn't know where he is."

Ted interrupted, "But, Grandma, why not?"

"It's OK not to understand now, Ted. Someday when you're older, you will. Now let's all have a snack. Grandma bought some big juicy strawberries today while you were at school. How about we cut up some to put on top of a big dish of vanilla ice cream?"

"So we'll have a Sunday and it's only Wednesday, right, Grandma?" Tom squealed. Then the two boys jumped up and ran after Naomi into the kitchen laughing. On the way Naomi could hear her Lovely Lily, her Flower stirring in her bed in the room above. She wondered if there was any way her daughter had overheard what the three of them had just talked about. She hoped against hope she hadn't.

But that wasn't the worst question Naomi had to answer. One day as she prepared dinner when Ted was on the verge of puberty several years after his Mother died, he asked out of the blue, "Grandma, was Mom a prostitute?"

"Where did you ever get that idea, Ted?"

"Some guys at school heard their Moms saying she was always having men in her bedroom. I remember Tom and I used to hear odd noises when we were trying to go to sleep. We never said anything then, but now we know what was really happening."

"I'm so sorry, Ted. You guys have had so much on your plates to deal with all these years. Your Mom had many problems, but she loved you and your brother very much. Never forget it no matter what anyone tells you about her."

"Did those men give her money too, Grandma?"

"That's beyond the point now, Ted."

"No, it isn't, Grandma. Tom and I want to know."

"Even if she did, that's water over the dam. There's nothing you can do about it. Now let's just put this discussion behind us. Your Mom was sick from too much alcohol among other things, but she loved you two a lot and always wanted the best for you."

"Then why did she do all those bad things?!"

"I told you, Ted, she had a lot of problems. That's the end of the story. Now call your brother. Dinner's ready. Don't forget to do your homework afterwards."

With all her being Naomi hated even thinking about all those sad days and nights. Having to put her poor Lovely Lily, her Flower in the ground with a pauper's funeral. Having hardly any money to raise her grandsons so there certainly was none left for a fancy casket or burial plot for their Mother. Oh, how difficult it was to remember and relive those sad days. How terrible it had been for her young grandsons to live through them too!

Naomi tried to calm herself down by thinking about the life of the old nun on today's cruise again. Sure, she didn't seem all "there" most of the time, but she had many people to take care of her. From her limited perspective she really believed Sister had it made and then some. All she could think about was how lucky that old nun always was and, on the other hand, how damn unlucky she'd always been! It just wasn't fair!

She sank into her recliner and put her feet up. They always hurt an awful lot after a busy afternoon working the luncheon cruise. Today they felt much worse because of those damn crazy teenagers and their music still pounding, pounding, pounding throughout her body! How she detested that music! And that "scratching" noise, did they really call that music? It just hurt her ears.

A vision of those kids dancing on the boat flashed across her memory. She never got to go dancing when she was that young. She never had a chance to learn how to jitterbug. It was war time and she had a job in a factory ten hours a day just like old Rosie the Riveter on the war posters. What horrible noise from all of the huge machines and the deadening monotony of the work! Some days she just wanted to die when she got home. No time for any fun and games and certainly none for frivolous dancing or even going out on dates to a movie or a restaurant like an ordinary young woman. It was almost like she was stuck working in the coal mines of her nightmare.

Except in her imagination of course.... Ah, there she was the lovely young and only daughter of a wealthy business man. Attending Coming Out Parties. Her own, of course, first. Enjoying big Birthday bashes. Dancing the nights away with tall handsome men. Wearing long designer gowns accented with diamond and jade jewelry. Flying to far away exotic islands for long lazy vacations in the sun. None of her wishes ever going unfulfilled. Her Daddy, fawning over her always calling her his "Little Darling" and she always telling him, "Oh, Daddy, I love you bunches!"

And her Mommy, her beautiful young Mommy, brushing her long blond hair a hundred times every night right before kissing her three times - once on her forehead and then once on each cheek as she crooned softly with her lovely lilting voice, "Dearest Naomi, sleep with the angels. They will protect you throughout the night. I love you, Honey Dear!" Oh, what a wonderful life that would have been!

Naomi also imagined her Lovely Lily her Flower growing into a beautiful young woman with an abiding interest in art, an honor roll student, a good girl with equally fine friends who enjoyed each other's company but never crossed over the line into alcohol and certainly not into drugs. She could see images of her daughter in her mind's eye dressed up in a stunning prom gown of pink and white lace, then in a black graduation gown with her college summa cum laude diploma in her hand, then in a designer wedding gown with a long elegant train.

Her real life, though, was absolutely the opposite of all that. Hand-me-downs ripped and stained. Shoes with holes in them. No toys or books of her own. Yelled at a lot. Pummeled by her foster or adoptive parents even if they had the least problem with her. Not allowed to go out with the other girls and guys because she always had to work. Work. Work! Even before she was old enough to have a paying job, she was always the Cinderella of the House, having to pick up even after the birth kids of the family and take their parents' severe scolding if she did anything they didn't like. The worst one was a spoiled brat named Princess May. At every chance she got, she tattled on her for insignificant things like being in the bathroom for more than a few minutes or not coming to help her find her shoes as soon as she yelled for her.

One day she went so far as to accuse her of stealing a twenty dollar bill from her Mother's purse which Naomi had seen her take herself. But it was the spoiled little angel of the family's word against hers so she caught the wrath of Princess May's Mother. How sore her behind was for weeks from the hard whipping with a wooden spoon she gave her! She would never forget that injustice and abuse and most of all how Princess May always sneered at her from then on, sticking her long fang-like tongue out at her every time she saw her!

How drastically different her succession of foster Mothers and then her step Mother were from her Imaginary Mother! None of them really cared about her and certainly none of them ever loved her for herself. It seemed to her that they only worried about how much money she cost them and how much she could bring home to them from whatever job she had. They never hugged her or solaced her in any way if they ever even realized she was in need. She was not much more than a big crumb on the floor to them no matter how long she worked, how much money she gave them, how hard she tried to be a good foster or adoptive daughter.

Even when she was old enough to get a job like babysitting and was paid, it didn't matter because she couldn't keep any of the money anyway. She had to give all of it to her foster parents or to her step parents because otherwise they would hit her with whatever was in their reach at the time. The woman sometimes a spatula or a wooden spoon like Princess May's Mother used. The man his leather belt or his clenched fist.

She didn't recall any time when she felt a Mother's love in her life except right before her Lovely Lily, her Flower was born. A kind nun watched over her while she was living in the Midtown Mission for Women. She was more a Mother to her in all the real ways that count than any of the other women called foster or step Mother. She was so lucky to have met her for she truly cared for her. That made all the difference in her life. All these years later she wished she could thank her again and again.

How unbearably tired she always was when she got home after whatever job she had to whatever foster family had reluctantly taken her in or, worse, her step parents, almost all of them just to earn some extra dollars. She nearly died each night from pure, unadulterated exhaustion.

She felt that same total exhaustion today so many decades later. Would she ever in her life get a decent night's sleep? Not with her grandsons coming in and out at all hours or up studying into the moonlight. Four hours of actual sleep was the most she got on a good night when her recurrent nightmares eased up a bit. She never knew in advance when that would happen so each night as she lay her head on her pillow, she said a quick prayer Sister taught her. A Hail Mary, her favorite. All she remembered today was the first line, "Hail Mary, full of grace, the Lord is with thee."

She always had so many damn things to do. After all, she couldn't expect the boys to help much with their full class schedules and part-time jobs to help pay their tuition for graduate school. What she made on the boat was so little, but they needed every single penny just to survive. An occasional tip really came in handy too. She did get a small Social Security check every month which fortunately helped to keep them off Welfare. Naomi was thankful for that.

But those lucky nuns never had to worry about money. No, all their needs and desires would always be provided and then some. They didn't have to work like she did day and night, night and day. Furthermore, she couldn't even imagine having a birthday celebration on a luncheon cruise, no less, like that old nun had today. Never in her whole sad life had anyone thrown even an ordinary birthday party for her.

She kicked off her shoes. She'd been standing on her feet morning, noon and night since she was barely a teenager. Not dancing like those kids on the boat to that loud and crazy music they seemed to like so much. Always on her feet for what seemed like days at a time whether in a factory, restaurant, bar and grille, department store or luncheon cruise boat like now. Oh, if only everything had been different in her life.... If only her Mother hadn't died.... If only she had grown up in one really loving family.... Oh, how wonderful her life would have been.

Wonderfully, though, she did have a few glorious days of real rest when her Lovely Lily, her Flower was born. How old was she then? Naomi wracked her brain trying to remember. It seemed like a century ago and really was as far as she was concerned. She had pushed memories about her daughter during those days so far back in the closet of herself, she really had to ponder for many minutes to retrieve her age from all the difficult remembrances pushed back in there.

Then all of a sudden it did come raging back to her like a

truck hitting her head on. She was twenty five then. A difficult time with no husband. No Alan to support her through all the months of waiting. And no one with her during her long hours in labor either. How forlorn and isolated she had felt! Today it made her cry thinking how selfish she was complaining about giving birth without Alan beside her when she had been told he had died alone so far away. Oh how much she still missed him even now half a century later!

How could any of those nuns ever feel that same kind of desolation? After all, they always had each other around them all the time. That "Birthday Girl" today just had to open her mouth or even just move a muscle, and someone was right there to help her. What a fine life she and all those nuns had!

Oh but she had those special hours and days after her Lily was born that they would never know. What joy! The only true joy of her life. Her Lovely Lily, her Flower, a delicate baby weighing barely six pounds with very light skin that was so transparent she could almost see clear through it. From the first days of her life, she seemed to smile up at her every time she nursed her. Oh what a fine daughter her Lovely Lily, her Flower was at the very beginning of her life!

Her Lovely Lily her Flower was such an adorable little girl! Naomi remembered how she loved her first baby doll, a soft and cuddly newborn that looked real enough. She could see her dress and undress it, caress it holding it carefully in her arms, even bathe it. She slept with it in her arms every night and carried it around with her throughout most of each day. She named her "Baby." Naomi sighed deeply, "Oh what a sweet, sweet memory!"

One thing was sure that old nun with the crooked headpiece would never know how happy a child of her own could make her!

Then again she'd never know all the heartbreak one could also bring her either. Heartbreak on Heartbreak on Heartbreak! Naomi's eyes filled with tears which gushed down her face. She hastily wiped them away refusing to relive all that pain today. She only wanted to revel in the joy of remembering the good times. Holding her Lovely baby Lily, her Flower in her arms again. Feeling her feed on her breasts and smile up at her. Caressing her softer than soft baby skin just relishing the peace, the contentment, the love she felt for her despite... No, she vowed she would not let those excruciating memories bother her now. Not today!

She fell into a deep sleep in her favorite chair as though she was basking in her own biological Mother's love. In the love of the woman who left her world too soon. The Mother who never held her in her arms or nursed her or sang her to sleep with a fancy lullaby…

In her dream she was a little pigtailed girl of six running and jumping up into her beautiful young Mother's arms. Feeling her sweet kisses all over her face and neck. Smelling the pleasant lavender perfume on her body. Loving her so much, while knowing at the same time how much she loved her too.

Oh but then darkness! Pitch blackness like at the end of a movie before the lights go back on. Her Mother fading to a Shadow. Then to Nothing. Only Nothing. All her joy vanished. Her body and soul desolate and alone again. Still. Like forever....

Naomi awoke with a start fortunately for once with no conscious memory of the end of the dream/nightmare. Jumping up, she realized she had to get something ready for her grandsons to eat.

After a quick meal of a salad with macaroni and cheese, they each kissed her goodbye and hurried off to their jobs, Ted's at the Campus Grille and Tom's at the Ice Cream Shoppe down the street. Each only made around minimum wage at these places, but they knew only too well like their Grandma that every single dollar counted.

After they left and Naomi cleaned up the kitchen, she fell into her soft recliner to watch one of her favorite sitcoms, but she couldn't concentrate on it. The jokes didn't make her laugh and the story line seemed sillier than usual to her. Flicking off the TV, she sat staring out the window. She couldn't get the face of that old nun with the crooked headpiece out of her mind. How she envied her! She would always be taken care of and in the end be given a proper funeral. She knew that much about religious communities. They took care of their own from Day One to Day End.

But who would take care of Naomi in her advanced age when she could finally stop going to work all the time? Whenever she got real sick or mentally confused like that strange old nun? Who would take care of her then? Sure, her grandsons would do whatever they could, but would anyone else care about her? She thought about all of the parents she had lived with and especially about her abusive adopted parents who disowned her when she got pregnant by their only son. None of them would ever reach out to help her even if they knew where she was now.

No, she only had Ted and Tom if they were even still around when she needed them most. Of course, she knew her "two boys" she loved more than her own life loved her a lot as well. Yet tonight nothing could solace her.

Chapter 5

A New Life

Oh, if only Alan's parents hadn't forced him to enlist in the Army after they found out she was carrying his child. If only he hadn't been sent to fight in that insane Korean War on the other side of the world which might as well have been on another planet as far as she was concerned. If only he had lived to return home and be a family with her and her Lovely Lily, her Flower. Maybe with him as her Father, she wouldn't have gone off the deep end the way she did.

Oh how she missed her Alan, the Love of Her Life! How she so yearned to be held in his arms again. To feel his skin touch hers. To glory in their togetherness. Sometimes she felt she could reach out in bed and hold him. Caressing. Swooning in a passionate release with him. And then simply go to sleep wrapped in his fondness. Oh, how she deeply yearned!

But no! He had to die in that godforsaken place without her there to hold his hand. With no one to comfort him. Alone. Coming home in a box. She couldn't even go to his funeral because his parents told her she wasn't welcome.

Months later when she called to tell them about her Lovely Lily, her Flower's birth, they never even asked to see their granddaughter. It was as though they refused to admit she had been conceived at all, angry because they believed her Mother had seduced their perfect son so she would get pregnant to trick him into marrying her. Naomi knew they considered her little better than a disgusting hunk of white trash. They only took her in, only chose to adopt her years before, as Alan reluctantly confided in her one day, because they wanted to impress their new pastor with their wonderful good deed reaching out to a poor young girl who had lived with one foster family after another for most of her life. If only that minister knew. If that minister only knew Naomi probably would have fared so much better on her own instead of in their house as the Cinderella and the Nurse Maid and the Whipping Board all rolled into one. If only that minister had known the truth!

Of course, lots of people would wonder why she stayed with that dysfunctional family for so many years. The only answer she had in retrospect was she had no other viable option. She'd graduated from high school only by the skin of her teeth, studying at odd times during whatever afterschool job she had or staying up reading with a flashlight under the covers at night so her parents wouldn't find out somehow and punish her. All she really knew how to do was cook and clean and take care of young children. The only possessions she had were several well-worn skirts and blouses, threadbare underwear, a thin coat, a pair of shoes and socks - all castoffs a transient would probably reject. Looking back, she knew she had to take whatever abuse her adoptive parents levied on her just so she'd have a place to live. What did she know about homeless shelters all those years ago. She wasn't even sure there were any then.

It was Thanksgiving in the early 50s when Alan came home from college that they got together for the first time. He was twenty-one, she three years older. She'd stayed with his family even after "becoming an adult" because she had little education, no special skills and nowhere else to go. In the beginning Alan was just trying to console her by holding her affectionately in his arms after yet another hateful tongue-lashing or worse from his Mother or Father. Naomi didn't deserve his parents' abusive treatment since she worked so hard for them day in and day out. He hated hearing her being berated and yelled at and, most of all, beaten by them.

What were only fleeting attempts in the beginning to make her feel better and soothe the pain of his parents' abuse soon evolved into something more. She could almost remember every touch, every sensation, every emotion she felt that first night....

She had had a particularly trying day working at a small restaurant for a meager salary and usually meager tips no matter how or what she did to fulfill every wish or whim of every diner. When she fell into the house at 11 pm that night, Alan's parents were waiting for her.

"Well, Missy, where were you all this time? You better not have met up with some guy instead of coming right back here!" In her mind's eye Naomi saw red venom dripping from her Stepmother's mouth as she yelled at her.

"You're right, dear. This damn little tart better stop flirting with all those men and start working harder to get better tips or I'm going to have to...." her Stepfather added, his hairy fists clenched ready to pound her back for the hundredth time.

Naomi winced and softly said, "Here's your money. I'm going to bed now. I start tomorrow at eight. The manager's adding breakfast."

"OK, then. Good! More money coming our way. Make sure we get it. You better get into bed right away then. And be out of here by 7:30 in the morning so you're not late, you hear?" her Stepmother bellowed as Naomi hurried from the room imagining her licking her lips as she thought about the new outfit she'd buy with the extra money she'd be getting from her.

Aspiring capitalists, they invested in Naomi so she could

produce income for their consumer-obsessed lifestyles. The Larsons ascribed to the egoist Ayn Rand's belief that "The ladder of success is best climbed by stepping on the rungs of opportunity," which in this case was achieved by stepping on Naomi to squeeze every bloody cent out of her.

All Naomi wanted to do when she got to her room and locked the door, her one consolation and piece of peace, was to drop in her bed and die for seven hours.

Suddenly someone was talking to her....

"I'm so sorry about my parents. If I could apologize every minute of every day, it wouldn't be enough. You don't deserve such treatment from them." Alan had ducked into her room and waited for her.

For the next hour the two melded into each other's beings as though they'd been together for a lifetime. They'd had enough anticipation from the months before when he just hugged her or caressed her bruises after a bad run in with his Father. They were both ready to be together fully even though this was her first time.

They slept the rest of the night in each other's arms, Alan being sure to slip out to his room right before dawn so Naomi wouldn't be accused of leading him on. After all, he needed her maybe more than she needed him. He'd been living with his parents from hell for all his life.

Naomi knew instinctively that her Lily, her Flower started

to be that night. No matter what happened to her the rest of her life, she'd always have a piece of Alan with her. Or so she thought or believed at the time....

Very quickly she found herself falling in love with Alan. One night he told her he loved her too and wanted to be with her for the rest of his life. How ecstatic Naomi had felt then!

However, when she thought about how things actually turned out, she scowled at Old Man Fate's mean twists and turns. How could she and Alan have been such "star-crossed lovers" like that couple Romeo and Juliet whose story she had watched one night on TV? They at least died more or less together, but she had to go on living without her Alan.

He was in his senior year at business school when the word got out that she was with child. One of his parents' friends saw Naomi leaving the local doctor's office. The woman knew the receptionist and squirmed out of her the reason why she was there.

"You selfish, ungrateful wench!" her Stepmother screeched at the top of her lungs when she heard the news. "Taking advantage of our dear only son! How dare you get pregnant just to hold onto him after all we've done for you!"

Then her Stepfather piped in bellowing, "Alan's going into the Army next week so you'll never see him again. God's going to punish you for seducing our son. Don't you ever forget it!"

He glared at her then as she remembered one of the worst of the many times he hurt her. She was only thirteen when he mercilessly whipped her with his wire hair brush only because she supposedly lost a quarter on the way to pick up some bread at the market. Naomi could still feel how hard he hit her. She couldn't sit without being in terrible pain for weeks. If only she had told someone. At the time, though, she was convinced no one would believe her anyway. Mr. Larson was such an upstanding member of the community, deeply involved with the Church and other religious charities, and she was just a dumb young kid he so "kindly adopted out of the goodness of his heart," as she once overheard him tell his friend on the phone. So she realized at that very young age she had no choice but to learn how to steel herself to take whatever abuse he or his wife gave her.

There were other times too. Times when she didn't give him all the money he expected from her jobs. Or when she didn't do all the housework exactly as his wife had told her. Times when she got a bad report from school because she was caught dozing in class or came to school five minutes late. In all these situations and others she chose not to recall now, he would pull off his leather belt and beat her until she was like a limp weed on his lap. But she never begged him to stop. Never cried out. Never gave him the least indication that he hurt her so badly.

But that didn't mean he didn't hurt her. There were days when she couldn't sit for a few minutes without being in extreme pain. Days when her arms were so sore she could hardly pick up a pen or do her part-time work after school. Through it all she learned how to remain as calm and as unfeeling as she could every time he came after her with his belt or, worse, his fist.

His wife, her ugly obese Stepmother, sometimes mistreated her even more dreadfully! She hardly ever beat her though. All these years later Naomi believed that was because she didn't want to mess up her gaudy manicures. No, she'd do something worse instead - berate her into the ground calling her "a lazy dog" or "a no good girl who only cared about herself" or a sneak and a liar and....

The day her adoptive parents found out about her pregnancy, she happened to be in the kitchen when she overheard them talking. She hid in the pantry to listen but was so sorry afterwards that she did.

"That ungrateful bitch! Seducing our Alan and purposely getting pregnant! Imagine!"

"Well she's not staying here for us to raise that little brat."

"So what are we going to do about Alan? He'll want to marry that dirty trash and leave us. I won't stand for that!"

"Calm down, Erma. We'll think of something. I agree she took advantage of him because she knew he'd want to do the honorable thing and marry her. We have to get rid of her to protect him."

"But how, Fred? We must do something."

"First, of course, we throw her out of here. Then..."

"We could send him to graduate school."

"No, too much damn money!"

"OK. How about...."

"Wait a damn minute. I got it. I'll get him to enlist in the Army!"

"Oh, Fred, I absolutely hate that idea. He'll be shipped off to that Korean War before we know it. And then who knows what will happen to him. And anyway how can we make him do that if he doesn't want to? Oh, my little boy!"

"Be reasonable, Erma. You're thinking with your damn heart, not your mind!"

"But, Fred!"

"No, Erma, this is the best plan. We'll tell him right now. He's already made his bed so he'll damn well have to sleep in it!"

When "Erma Blabberamma" as Naomi called her to herself, left the room, Naomi stayed in her hiding place to hear whether Alan would stand by her or let his parents continue to run his life. Unfortunately, when all three were in the room, their voices became quite subdued so she could only make out bits and pieces of what they said. "...enlist...no life with her...on return...sports car...why?...she's no good...will ruin you...she's leaving too...wants no part of you...."

At this lie Naomi almost gave herself away by screaming, "No! No!" But she covered her mouth biting her lips until they bled. The sound of intermittent words persisted. "....must leave...now...no seeing that bitch...do us proud...."

Alan stormed out of the room then as Fred said to Erma words Naomi strained to hear, "...no intention of buying that loser any car...even if he's lucky to come home...."

It was then that Naomi threw up on the floor but didn't care. She was going to be out of this hell hole before anyone saw her again so someone else could clean up her parting gift.

How did Alan let Erma and Fred bamboozle him like that? As though the promise of a car was worth more than she was! And that was only if he survived the war! As far as she ever knew, he left the house without ever knowing about his child she was carrying. He never would have given in to his parents if he had known, would he?

What Naomi couldn't have known was that Erma had motioned to Fred at the beginning of their conversation that she knew she was in the pantry listening to them.

Chapter 6

Another Flower

Desolate and in near despair, Naomi slipped out of the "House of Abuse" none the wiser about Alan's parents' subterfuge. She left with her meager possessions in a lone bag before they had the satisfaction of throwing her out. Fortunately, she had squirreled away five tens from her work of the past year so she wasn't entirely without resources. For that she was grateful. But heartsick, she didn't know where she'd lay down her head that night or how she'd care for the child growing inside her in the months to come....

"No!" Naomi yelled at herself while sitting in her little apartment so many years after her escape, "No more thinking about all this bad stuff! The one and only one good thing from it all was I met and fell in love with that horrible couple's son, my Alan, the Love of My Life! And my Lovely Lily, my Flower

117

came to me because of him."

No matter how hard she tried, though, she couldn't forget how absolutely bereft she felt the day she left Alan's parents' house without even letting her say goodbye to their son. Did he even know she was carrying his child? Had anyone told him? She hadn't told him yet because she was waiting for the "Almighty Perfect Moment." Oh, how she despised herself now for that decision! Maybe, just maybe, if she had told him before his parents found out, Alan could have arranged for them to get their own place together so they could be a family. But no, she blew it! Old Man Fate, who always kept her down, got her again Big Time! She had nowhere to turn. No one to go to. No one to help a now homeless girl unmarried and several months pregnant.

Naomi relived all the heart wrenching pain she felt as she walked the streets of the city trying to figure out what to do that earth-shattering day. Trying to decide how she'd take care of her baby if she was lucky enough to be born healthy despite all the abuse Naomi had suffered in her adoptive parents' home. As she continued to wrack her brain about what she should do, where she could turn, how she and her tiny one were going to survive, she felt like her feet were falling off they hurt so badly. She was so dead tired she could have just stretched out on the sidewalk and gone to sleep, but she had her unborn child to think about so she knew she had to keep on keeping on.

Just as she was about to give up, she could have sworn

she heard her baby crying, "Help me, Mommy. Help me!" Then as though a magnet lifted her eyes, she saw a sign on the building right in front of her which read "Midtown Mission for Women." Almost falling into the door, she looked up at the sky and cried out, "Oh Alan, me and our little one are going to be all right now!"

As the months passed, if he ever attempted to send her letters from the war zone, she never received any. Most likely his parents destroyed any that might have come to her from him. When she attempted to send Alan letters herself, they always came back to her stamped "Undeliverable."

Wherever he was, whatever had happened to him, he had altogether disappeared from her life and that was that. There was absolutely nothing she could do about it now all these decades later. She had somehow survived without him or any other man for that matter since then. She had put all her attention and love in her Lovely Lily, her Flower and her two grandsons. She had unselfishly dedicated her whole life only to them....

For the rest of her pregnancy, she was very fortunate to live and earn her keep at the mission by helping out in the kitchen cutting up vegetables, cleaning the huge ovens and the rooms and serving meals to the other residents. A nice nun with a strange name had taken her in. She couldn't remember her name no matter how hard she tried. But she did recall how kind that nun had been to her. She never yelled at her for getting "in the family way" without being married. She never put her down for being a sinner. She never laid a hand on her to punish her for being "a bad girl." No, she just took good care of her. Took her under large wings like she was an real Angel which she certainly seemed to be then and still was to Naomi all these years later. She had saved her life and her Lovely Lily, her Flower's too.

Yes, Sister was especially nice to her from the minute she walked in the door of the shelter. Like a human guardian angel she took Naomi under her wings so that from minute one she felt at home within the confines of the crowded noisy building which needed painting rather badly. Sister set her up in a room next to hers, showed her where all the facilities were and assured her she and her baby would be well taken care of.

One morning when she was about seven months along, Naomi remembered waking up and seeing Sister sitting nearby watching her. She couldn't imagine why. Sitting up in bed, she asked, "Is everything OK, Sister?"

"I'm fine, my dear one. I came in to wake you for breakfast but watching you sleep I couldn't help imagining your little one kicking as it seemed to wake up. I hope you aren't upset with me."

"How could I be, Sister? You've been my salvation all these months. I don't know how I would have survived without your support. You know what I really, really wish, though? I wish you could come with us when we have to leave here.

Wouldn't that be wonderful?"

"Indeed it would be, my dear, but I have a commitment to my community through Holy Obedience to work here. As much as I would love to act as your child's Grandmother, I..."

"Oh, I know, Sister. Still it would be so lovely if...."

"Well, God's ways are not our ways, Naomi, or vice versa. And so it's been ordained that you go your way and I stay here to minister to other pregnant girls like you."

"And they'll each be so lucky to have you as I have been. Oh, Sister, I couldn't have survived if not for you! You've saved my life and my baby's and given me true hope for the future."

"Now, now, don't go giving me all the credit, Naomi. Remember God takes care of His own. St. Paul said, 'To those who love God, all things work together unto good.' Never forget that, my dear little one."

Another day stood out in her memory. Sister had been helping the eight months pregnant Naomi to change her clothes - maternity garments the shelter had let her wear. After sitting back down on her bed, Naomi noticed Sister staring at her with an odd faraway look in her brown eyes though she didn't think anything about that at the time. Taken aback by the nun's apparent fixation, she asked her, "Is anything wrong? You look so sad."

She didn't answer but when Naomi tried to press her further, all the nun replied was, "I can't really explain it to you, my dear. Only after your child is.... " She trailed off into silence.

Returning from her thoughts, Sister asked Naomi in an upbeat sounding voice, "Why don't you get ready for dinner? The Cook told me we're having a special dessert tonight - your favorite peach pie."

Yes, it was a strange conversation Naomi only recalled years later after she found a job at a local department store when her Lovely Lily, her Flower was barely a year old. They could finally move into their own small apartment, a place where she still lived today with her two grandsons. But even then what the nun had said made her wonder what she was thinking about at the time. What did that nun know that she didn't? How could that old nun know anything about children? She was dedicated to God or as some said married to him. She heard that one of the vows she took was the vow of chastity which meant she could never be with a man or marry him or have his child.

If only Sister could have come to live with her and her baby girl. Maybe she wouldn't have lost whatever religion she gained from her over the months at the shelter.

One extremely bad morning when neither she not her Lily, her Flower slept much, she tried to reach Sister at the shelter. The girl at the main desk told her sister had been reassigned to teach at one of the community's high schools. When she asked where and for a forwarding address, she was told, "That information is not available." Horrified, she sank to the floor.

How could Sister's superior do this to her? How was she going to survive without even being able to talk to Sister on the phone? She was doing such good work at the shelter. She was really needed there but apparently more somewhere else taking care of teenagers in a classroom.

As Naomi continued to think about those days long ago, she realized her hold on anything holy or religious went out the proverbial window after Sister left the shelter. She didn't even get to say goodbye to her and thank her one last time for the many ways she helped her especially for being the only true friend she'd ever had. What kind of a supposed good and great God could do that to her? Why did he take away this woman she loved so much? This woman who was more her Mother than her biological one who died so long ago. And why did that supposed great and good God also take away her Alan, the only man she could ever love?

Naomi talked to her baby's Father now as though he was right in the room with them, "Oh, Alan, how I would love you to see our little darling baby, our Lovely Lily, our Flower. She is so beautiful and so delicate with very soft blond hair. Oh why did I have to lose you and Sister too? Does God hate me that much to take away my own Mother and give me all those terrible substitutes especially Erma? What have I ever done that was so wicked to have suffered so much?"

Then she remembered vividly that from somewhere inside

herself, she heard Sister whisper encouragingly, "Take heart, dear one. God loves you and will protect you like even the sparrows in the sky and the lilies in the field. Cherish your darling Lily. She will make all the difference in your life. Be of good faith always. God will take care of you. Be assured of that."

As the nun's words evaporated into the air, Naomi cuddled her Lovely Lily, her Flower closer to her heart and sang her a lullaby. Then she kissed her on both cheeks and carefully put her in her crib as her teardrops flowed down on top of the baby's pink blanket.

As she was falling asleep, she thought about Sister's favorite lines from Jesus at the Last Supper, "You now indeed have sorrow, but I will see you again and your heart shall rejoice and your joy no man shall take from you." Sister had explained to her that she believed Jesus said these reassuring words first to his Apostles sitting at the table with him, next to his Mother and Mary Magdalen and finally to all of us. In this way Naomi felt He was speaking to her directly, telling her she'd see Sister again and she'd have joy no one could take away form her. She could only wish that with all her heart.

Oh but what was the odd name of that nun who helped her at that place for unwed Mothers? Out of the wild blue it came to her in a bright revelation... Sister Eustacia!

Naomi jumped up from her bed with a start, her heart pounding like a thousand drums inside her chest. Didn't that old nun with the crooked headpiece who was celebrating her ninety-fifth birthday on the boat today have that same odd name? Was there any way she could have been the one who came to her rescue before her Lovely Lily, her Flower was born? She had no way to know. Or did she? She could go to the Retirement Home and ask to talk to the nun. The address of the place would be on the records from today's cruise.

Naomi fell asleep anxious for the next day to come when she'd find out where to go to talk to the old nun. To thank her after all these years if she was, in fact, the same one who had saved her life and her Lovely Lily, her Flower's too. That night she slept soundly with no nightmares marring her peaceful rest.

She found the address of Saint Clara's Retirement Home the next day as soon as she got to work, but the place was located so many miles outside the city, she had to wait a whole week until she had enough time off from work and could figure out what bus line would take her there. She had high hopes that the old nun would turn out to be the one who was her Salvation when she was down and out and pregnant so many years ago.

But when an aide wheeled Sister Eustacia into the visitor's lounge, Naomi wasn't so sure there would be any answers. Sister looked even more bewildered than she did on the boat the week before. Her eyes were bloodshot and not focusing and she kept mumbling, "She can't be dead."

Naomi reached over and touched her arm to get her

attention, but the old woman just stared at her as though she was from Mars or another galaxy. Then she asked her weakly in quick succession, "Who are you? Do I know you? How'd you get in here? What do you want?"

"Sister, don't you remember me? I was your waitress on your birthday cruise last week."

"No, I....What cruise? Oh, do you mean the one on the Ile de France across the Atlantic Ocean to Paris?"

"No, Sister. On the boat on the Baltimore Harbor a week ago. Please try to remember."

"Oh yes! On the boat meeting James. Dancing the Charleston. Getting my hair bobbed. Putting on a pearly Flapper dress I borrowed. Rolling my stockings. Drinking lots of champagne. James' charming smile... What fun we had! But oh how very angry Father was when he found us alone together in bed!" Sister's eyes sparkled blue-green, almost seeming to change shades as she talked excitedly.

"Please, Sister. It was just a week ago. We were on a boat in the Baltimore harbor."

"The harbor in Baltimore? Oh yes, Baltimore. Worked in that town for a long time. Took care of a lot of people. Taught a lot of teenagers too."

"You're on the right track now, Sister, so can you remember a pregnant girl you took in and cared for at the Midtown Mission for Women? It's me Naomi Renalt. I had my baby daughter, my Lovely Lily, my Flower while I was there. You were an angel who took both of us under your wing and were so kind to us. Please try to remember, Sister."

"So long ago. So many years. So many faces. So many I don't... But I remember James with his blue-green eyes. Oh how Father hated him for what he did to me!"

"Please, Sister Eustacia, it means so much to me. I think you might be the nun who saved my life and my Lovely Lily, my Flower's too."

"But I don't know anyone named Lily. I'm Mary."

"Lily was my daughter, Sister. Who's Mary?"

"Mary? Why that's me, of course. So you have a daughter too?"

"Had one. She died."

"So did mine. They told me."

"Who are you talking about, Sister?"

"My little baby girl."

"But...."

"So, so long ago. A different place and time. Sent away. Lost my little... Oh so terrible!" Sister Eustacia started to wail now, her frail body heaving uncontrollably.

Before Naomi could struggle up from her chair to try to comfort her, a young aide scurried to the old nun's side from out of nowhere seemingly. "Oh, I'm so sorry. Sister hasn't been feeling well especially during the past week. Ever since her birthday celebration on that boat, her mind's been playing all kinds of tricks on her making her more upset than usual. I'll take Sister back to her room to lie down."

"Oh, I guess that's best. Thank you for meeting with me, Sister. Goodbye."

Naomi patted the nun's liver spotted hand as the elderly woman's head sank down to her chest. When her wheelchair passed her, Naomi thought she heard her mumble, "No, my baby isn't dead!"

Naomi left the building more confused than she was when she arrived. All the way home on the bus, she thought about Sister Eustacia's strange ramblings. Though they didn't help her to know whether or not she was the nun who saved her life at the mission many years ago, Naomi sensed what she kept mumbling about James' eyes was meant to tell her something Sister knew that she should know. But then again none of what Sister had told her really made any sense. She obviously didn't know what she was saying. It was very hard and so sad to try to talk to a person so out of their mind. Apparently, she had one of those diseases - senility or Alzheimer's. Aren't they about the same?

Naomi was stymied. The old nun's mind was like several boxes of puzzles that had been spilled all over the floor. None of the pieces fit together; all of them were so mixed up they were almost impossible to sort out. What a poor, poor woman that old nun is! To be stranded most of the time in some nebulous long ago fantasy past without having any kind of real hold on the present. Naomi certainly couldn't envy her being in that condition because she felt she herself was on the way to that very same place.

When she got back to her apartment, her ears were assailed by the noise of the hip-hop music blaring from her grandsons' room. She made out just a few lines of the lyrics, "I'm bringing sexy back.// Who's your sexy now?// Get your sexy now." She never cared for that music and today liked it even less because it distracted her from trying to figure out why that old nun seemed so obsessed with James' blue-green eyes.

And what about the Ile de France Sister mentioned? Did she really travel on a boat by that name a long time ago? The Charleston, the hair bobbing and the Flapper clothes could be from when she would have been a young woman or maybe from a movie she had recently seen about that time. And who were James and Mary and the daughter Sister supposedly had who died like her Lovely Lily, her Flower? Could she have been talking from the lucid part of her brain when she mentioned them or only from her deluded mind? Could she have actually gotten pregnant before she became a nun and had a baby who then died?

Oh, how could any of this be true? Sister's been a nun for most of her life. Didn't one of her aides on the boat last week tell her that last year she celebrated almost eighty years in the convent? If she had a baby before she entered, she would have had to have been a teenage girl at the time. No, things like that didn't happen back then, did they? Or if they did, it was most unlikely. No, not Sister Eustacia!

Could the sad old soul just have been fantasizing about having a child and caring about someone named James? Why not? Imagine all those years living without a husband and children. Maybe what she'd missed out during all her years behind convent walls had finally gotten to her so that now in her old age, she yearned to have all of it. That explanation seemed logical to Naomi. She knew minds could play crazy tricks on people especially old ones. Hers certainly did. Even now there were times she felt Alan in her bed loving her to distraction even though she knew he was killed worlds away from her at least fifty years ago already. She'd feel him touch her so lovingly, running his fingers round and round her curves. He'd kiss her then with such passion and joy that never failed to nearly take her breath away. Ah, he was so fine to be with! And when he'd finally come inside her, she'd know again and again a wondrous high that sent her right off the edge of reality. Ah, her Alan. Her Alan! He was right here with her, wasn't he? Not in the ground somewhere. Not dead. Not gone. No!

Naomi's rational mind told her there was no way Alan could still be with her this way these many years later. But still her other minds, her fantasy mind, her going-crazy-with-loneliness mind or her almost-senile mind knew for sure her Alan had still been with her over the years.

She wondered if Sister Eustacia's mind was simply farther gone than hers. She seemed so tangled up, memories of the past entwined with her dreams and hopes that never came true, that she didn't know the difference between them anymore. Naomi remembered reading about people with "thin boundaries," those who weren't able to distinguish the difference between what was real or fantasy. Add that to the old nun's probable senility or Alzheimer's, how could anyone decipher the truths within the imaginations? The whole situation was so frustrating! Would she ever be able to find out for sure if the Sister Eustacia from the boat was actually the same one who saved her life and her Lovely Lily, her Flower's too?

Oh no. Looking at her watch, Naomi realized it was almost time to make dinner again. Hot dogs and baked beans and microwaved French fries today. While she was getting supper ready, she kept juggling some dates around in her head. If Sister Eustacia was ninety-five last week, then she was born in 1912. Since she herself was going on seventy-eight, she was born in 1929 when Sister would have still been a teenager. That could mean that she could almost be her...

No, of course not. Besides, Naomi's Mother had died long ago, right? And after all, Sister Eustacia's memory simply couldn't be trusted no matter what. She would have had to have a baby before she entered the convent or else while.... No, that's preposterous! Either way, she was told the baby died.

Naomi realized her mind was playing tricks on her now. Because of what the old nun had said about her supposed baby, she'd been remembering so much about her Lovely Lily, her Flower. Her mind was so confused! Sometimes a blur. Other times as real as if the past was still happening or happening over and over again. She hated to admit it even to herself but her mind was on its way to becoming just like the old nun's. Now that was an overwhelming thought! How would she and her grandsons cope with that? Would the two boys eventually be forced to "put her away" in one of those God-forsaken nursing homes? Oh no, dear Lord, no!

Her grandson's query, "Hey, Grandma, how soon is dinner?" grabbed Naomi out of her reverie of worst-case scenarios.

"In about ten minutes, Tom. Could you please turn down the volume in there? My old ears are hurting today."

"Sure thing, Grandma."

"What a good guy he is! They both are. Despite everything, I guess I've really been blessed," Naomi admitted to herself. They lost their Mother whom they hardly knew in their nine years before she died, but they grew up to be such great men. They loved their Grandma so much and always told her they appreciated everything she'd done for them. Yes, she'd really been blessed with them! And her Lovely Lily, her Flower would be so proud of them too if she knew they were both working on their Masters degrees in social work to help many people worse off than they were.

Despite her positive thoughts about Ted and Tom, that night Naomi had more trouble than usual falling asleep. Flashes of memories about her Lovely Lily, her Flower kept flowing across her memory like a movie on TV....

A beautiful curly haired two year old learning to go potty by herself. So proud when she did the first time that she radiated pure joy and squeaked in total delight. Getting ready for school the first day. So excited. Jumping up and down. Becoming a woman at only eleven. Not happy about it at first. Not liking the messiness. Graduating from eighth grade at the top of her class. Oh, she had so much going for her if only she hadn't.... Then dreadful memories like mean witches erased all the lovely ones on the edge of her consciousness before she finally fell asleep.

When her Lovely Lily, her Flower was a blossoming girl of twelve ironically only weeks before she actually needed the information, Naomi sat her daughter down for the "becoming a woman" talk. Lily insisted she knew all about the "old birds and bees" from the kids at school so she didn't need Naomi's input. Still her Mother persisted, "OK so, Miss Smarty Pants, you know all the facts, do you? Well, I'm here to tell you, there's so much more to all of this."

"OK, I'm listening," Lily reluctantly responded, bored out

of her mind.

"Here's the thing, Honey...."

"I hate it when you call me that, Mom! Just tell me whatever and hurry with it. I have lots of homework to do."

Naomi knew that was a lie. Her daughter's teacher were always complaining she never handed in her homework. Nevertheless, she continued, "Lily, one major thing you have to remember is as soon as you get your period, you can get pregnant. Save yourself for the Love of Your Life."

"Yeah, yeah. Until the Man of My Dreams turns up and we ride off into the sunset." Under her breath she added, "Whatever."

Naomi heard her comment but chose to ignore it. "So, Lily, remember your body's yours to decide what to do or not to do with it. Don't let any Tom, Dick or Harry do with it whatever he wants."

"OK OK Mom. I get it. Can I go do my homework now?"

Naomi was too tired to push the envelope any longer so she regretfully let her Lily, her Flower go to her room....

Years later she recalled every word of this conversation with great pain in her gut. How down had her Lovely Lily, her Flower already fallen during her pre-teen days? She'd heard about lots of young girls who did questionable things to be popular with certain guys. Her whole heart broke again just remembering. If she had been a better Mother, could she have saved her from herself and a devastating mix of sex, alcohol and probably drugs too? She didn't know but she always wondered, would everything be different? Would her Lovely Lily, her Flower still be alive so her sons would have a Mother? Would she herself have been spared the traumas of her final years? Would she have been saved from finding the drained and lifeless body as she did? Would everyone's lives have turned out better?

If she had only been a better Mother to her Lily, her Flower, then they could all be happy and full of life. Without a doubt. But why the hell did it turn out so wrong? Why did that damn holy God who Sister Eustacia always talked about give her such a repulsive life? Why does the "Man above" hate her and them so much?

Maybe if she had had a Mother, her real biological Mother, even if she had be to a single Mother like her, then none of the tragedies of her life would have happened. If only.... If only.... But, no, not for her!

Naomi remembered when her Lovely Lily, her Flower was barely a teenager and got in with the wrong crowd. She heard they danced to that raucous rock and roll Elvis Presley music at a place down the street. "You Ain't Nothing But a Hound Dog!" and "Jailhouse Rock!" blared through her memory where she could see the guys with their slicked back DA's some even wearing pink pegged pants, by damn! And the girls with their fancy hair flips and flared poodle skirts with wide white crinolines under them.

Naomi was almost certain that her Lovely Lily, her Flower started her unrestrained drinking and carousing with that crowd. First probably with Buddy, one of her first boyfriends, who always seemed to be hung over. He acted like he was really a big "cat." How sickening his smirk which always seemed plastered on his face was! Naomi hated answering the door whenever he came to pick up her daughter. Most of the time, though, he just leaned on the horn of his souped-up Chevy for her to come out. Naomi despised that even more.

Her stomach churned violently as she reluctantly relived the first time she got a call to pick up her Lovely Lily, her Flower from a local pub because she was blasted drunk causing a scene as she screamed hysterically and got sick all over the floor. When she pulled her up off the bar stool as she precariously swayed back and forth, she smelled beer she had apparently spilled down her shirt as she got more and more drunk. Laughing crazily as Naomi nearly dragged her out of the place, she warbled off key, "You are...my...special an...gel...sent from...up...above."

Naomi would never forget the horrible argument the next day when her Lovely Lily, her Flower finally sobered up. Sadly, it was the last extended conversation she was ever to have with her. Naomi made sure her grandsons were at a friend's place playing basketball before she sat her daughter down for this major heart to heart. She minced no words. "Lily, you've got to stop all this carousing and drinking. You're out of control!"

"Oh, Mom, so what if I have a few brews now and again. It's no big deal!"

"No, Honey, it really is a big deal! Don't ever forget that."

"Don't go patronizing me, Mom. I know what I'm doing."

"You do?"

"Sure, I just drink a bit and enjoy some fun with whoever whenever. That's all."

"But, Lily, it's become a habit with you and a very bad one. You're like a baby who needs their bottle!"

"Wow! What a God damned way you have of exaggerating everything I do, Mom!"

"No, I'm not exaggerating and you know it! You were so drunk last night you probably don't remember the scene you made spouting obscenities at the top of your lungs and then throwing up all over the place in front of the bartender and all the other people. You made a fool of yourself!"

"There you go again blowing every little stupid thing out of proportion! And anyway what do you care about what people saw or heard? I sure as hell don't!"

"Listen here, you're just out of control. I'd like to ground you for the next ten years!"

"What in the hell are you talking about now? I'm a grown woman with two sons. You're dreaming!"

"Oh, how I wish I were. I would so like to ground you and then give you a good spanking too. I wish your terrible behavior was just a great big joke. I wish you weren't ruining your life and messing up Tom and Ted's in the process. I wish...."

"Yeah. Yeah. I wish a lot of things too, Mom. I wish we didn't have to live here with you. I wish I had a husband so my boys would have a Father and we all lived together in a nice house and had a nice car and Tommy and Teddy could go to a better school outside the city instead of the damn crappy one down the street. Yeah, I wish for a lot too!"

"So if you're really serious about having all those things, when are you going to stop getting drunk every chance you get? When are you going to stop bringing home losers and pretending your sons don't know what's happening in your bedroom? You're messing up not only your life but also your boys! Grow up, damn it! You've been acting like some spoiled brat who isn't thankful for all she has. I'm working night and day trying to provide for all of us while you just...."

"So let me bow down to you now, your Majesty! You're so God damned perfect and I'm such a stupid loser! A bad Mother. A bad daughter. Go ahead say it!" At that the young woman stormed out of the room and ran out the front door red-faced and crying with anger. Naomi knew there was like an invisible rope pulling her to the bar down the street to find solace again in a bottle....

She swallowed hard blocking out any more bad memories about Lily. She just wasn't strong enough to relive any more terrible arguments with her now. If only she hadn't... No! No! She didn't want to think about her being stinking drunk anymore! She didn't want to see the grotesque older men she brought home who gave her money to make them happy. She couldn't let herself remember how her Lovely Lily, her Flower just seemed to wilt away throughout the rest of her short life thanks to all the booze and drugs and sex she lived for. She reluctantly remembered another night when she almost fell into the apartment sobbing and bleeding from her mouth after Buddy roughed her up for "cheating" on him. Her Lovely Lily, her Flower, spitting blood and whiskey all over the kitchen!

Of course, she realized it was in great part her fault. If only she had kept better tabs on her. If only she had been a better Mother. If only she hadn't been forced to work day and night jobs when she was growing up. If only... if only... if only. She should have done more to keep her away from all those temptations. She should have reached out to her counselors at school or maybe even to the minister at Church. She should have done so much more to save her. But the stark fact was that she didn't. She didn't do any of those things so her Lovely Lily, her Flower died an unspeakable death as a result.

Oh she was such a bad Mother! Naomi never even had a

Mother and yet her life was better than Lily's. At least she didn't get in with the wrong crowd and do all kinds of reprehensible things. Not that she ever had any time to do anything except work, work, work.

That night, she received a strange phone call.

"Hello, are you the Mother of Lily Renalt?"

"Who wants to know?"

"Well, let me say that my name's Lily Larson."

Naomi gasped and asked herself, "Larson? Larson? Wasn't that her Alan's last name?" Then she asked the stranger, "Lily, is your Father's name Alan?"

"As a matter of fact, it was."

"Was?"

"Yes, he passed away two weeks ago."

"Oh. I didn't know." Both were quiet for a moment.

"Is there some place we can meet where we can really talk?" Lily asked.

"Well, there's a diner on the corner of Bryan and Carl. It's called the Cozy Corner Diner. It's usually quiet at this hour with not many people."

"Oh and please call me Naomi."

"OK, I'll be there in a half hour Naomi. I have long blond hair and will be wearing a purple shirt."

"Fine, Lily. I look forward to talking with you."

Twenty minutes later a nervous wrinkled old woman

hugged the young blond woman. Naomi was overwhelmed. A piece of her Alan was sitting across from her! A second Lily! Questions flowed form her mouth in rushing waves.

"Lily, how did you find me? Did your Father ever tell you about me? What happened to him? Where does your Mother live?"

The young woman smiled slightly and playfully chided the older woman. "Whoa. Please slow down! First, let me tell you how I found you. It was very strange. You see as my Father was dying, he was growing delirious but he did say your name several times. Only your first name though. Unfortunately, my Mother had passed away ten years before so I couldn't ask her anything, not that she would have known about you. After Father's funeral I was going through his papers when I came across some assorted notes he wrote while in his 20's." Lily pulled a small notebook from her shoulder bag. As Naomi read Alan's words, she kept shaking her head slowly.

"N.R. ended up at the Midtown Mission for Women where I met S.E. and asked her to keep tabs on N. and our baby to come and keep me posted." Then a name Lily underlined and attached to the page a cancelled check for $5000 for the home.

"Oh, Lily, your Father was certainly my Alan, the Love of My Life. His parents adopted me when I was twelve. They were not very nice people abusing me in all kinds of ways. When your Father and I got together and then I found out I was pregnant with my Lovely Lily, my Flower, they threw me out of their house. That's when I ended up at the mission place."

"Oh, Naomi, I'm so sorry my Father didn't or couldn't stay with you. His Father supposedly wanted him to enlist in the Army but as far as we know, he wouldn't go along with it because he wanted to help people, not kill people. A kind old nun introduced him to Diana, his future wife. Apparently, my Mother never knew how you and Alan were connected."

"Please stop for a moment Lily. Could we just sit for a while as I try to let all of this into my pea brain?"

The two women drank several cups of coffee in mutual silence. Lily wanted to let Naomi continue their conversation when she was ready.

Suddenly, the old woman called out, "Why, Alan? Why?"

Was Naomi telling Alan she didn't understand what he had done or not done so many years ago? Naomi was discombobulated as the information Lily had just shared was disconcerting at best. Lily wondered how she could help her Father's old friend deal with his decisions, the main one being letting Naomi go out on her own.

"So your Father never told you and your Mother about me and his other Lily?"

"No, Naomi. As I said, I only found out about you from his notes. I called the home and squirreled out some information. One of the old timers remembered a nun who paid special attention to you and your baby daughter. When we put all the details together, they became like the final pieces of a big puzzle. Oh, Naomi, I am so glad this all worked out. My Father would be very happy I found you after all these years."

"Indeed, he would."

"Now I have a question for you. Where does your daughter, my half-sister, live?"

"Bad news, Lily. My own Lily, my Lovely One, my Flower died. About fifteen years ago."

"I'm so very sorry, Naomi. What happened?"

"She had a major alcohol problem among others. In the middle of the last night of her life, she came home drunk again, fell in the lobby or our apartment building, hit her head on a radiator and bled to death. I found her the next morning on my way to work. Oh how terrible! A sight I'll never forget!"

Lily nodded in empathy.

"One good thing, though, is that her twin boys Tom and Ted didn't find her. That would have been a million times worse for them..."

Wanting to change the subject, although not to a pleasant topic, she asked Lily, "Please tell me how did your Father die?"

"I watched him go downhill after he lost my Mother in childbirth along with their baby son. He was never the same. Now that I have met you and know about your Lily too, I wonder if he still blamed himself for letting you go especially if he ever found out about your Lily's death. I also wonder if he knew about his two grandsons. Oh, Naomi, isn't it strange how things turn out? How life goes. How weird events connect people and bring them together?"

"There's no doubt abut that! But I'll tell you what, I'm so very glad you tracked me down. Now I have a part of Alan after all these years."

"And I have a part of him left in a way too."

"Lily, will you do me the honor of becoming a member of my family? Meeting my Lily's sons. Becoming their long lost aunt."

"Of course. I'd be proud and very happy to do that, Naomi."

"It's agreed then. Will you come to dinner at our apartment on Friday at 7? I'll make sure the boys will be there to meet you."

"That sounds great, Naomi."

"Oh, wait a moment. Am I losing my mind or what? I never asked you what you do, if you're married and have any children."

"No apologies necessary. I work with handicapped kids, Naomi. I'm not married and until the past hour or so had no relatives. I'm so glad to have people I can now call family."

Lily reached across the table and squeezed Naomi's hands. Then they both slipped out of the booth at the same time.

Laughing and crying, they hugged each other for several minutes.

On her way home Naomi was glad that at least she knew what really happened to the Love of her Life even though she only had him for such a short time.

Later when she found the Obituary, it struck her with a force that almost knocked her down. There was no mention of his being in the Army, let alone any other branch of the military, but one fact jumped out of the newsprint at her; he had one surviving daughter also named Lily! Naomi was overwhelmed. Why did she ever believe Alan's parents? She should never have trusted anything that came out of their abusive mouths. They were repulsive imitations of good parents! Oh why did she ever let them cheat her out of being with Alan, The Love of Her Life?

Actually, against his parents' strict orders Alan had surreptitiously kept tabs on Naomi after she left their home. Of course, he knew she was pregnant with his child. He donated the significant amount of money his parents had bribed him to stay away from her to the place for women in need he saw her almost fall into. He talked to a very nice nun there who promised him she'd take his friend under her wing. Throughout the next seven months she kept him apprised of Naomi's well being, especially during her labor and the birth of their child. When he married years later, he insisted to his wife that their daughter be named Lily. Unbeknownst to anyone else, so named after his first child.

Downright distraught after reading Alan's Obituary,

Naomi sank back into a disturbed sleep tossing and turning throughout the night and into the early morning, a new nightmare haunting her unconscious mind....

Lily being slapped around by an overweight balding middle-aged man who called her "a lovely slut and whore." Then being thrown on the floor and spit on by a younger man with dishwater blond hair who looked like her boyfriend Buddy. Lily standing up and kicking him in the groin then screaming, "Mommy! Daddy! Help me. Please hurry!" Naomi working many miles away at an all-night diner oblivious to her daughter's cries.... and Alan nowhere to be found....

When Naomi dragged her weary body out of bed the next morning, a migraine pounded into her consciousness a hundred times louder than the music on the boat the week before or from her grandsons' room. She searched the apartment for aspirin but only found an empty bottle abandoned on a shelf in the bathroom. She had to take something to get herself going. Today a group of forty golfing buddies had reserved the whole boat. Once they started drinking, they'd get so noisy and demanding she'd be running around busier than ever for the whole afternoon. Still she needed the money so badly she knew she would smile and smile and wait on them hand and foot, foot and hand, hoping against hope they'd give her big tips to make all the pain and aggravation worthwhile.

If truth be told, she always felt like the men's slave the way they treated her. In fact, several reminded her of the horrible man who adopted her, Alan's Father. They sneered at her no matter how hard she tried to please them. She had to put on a real class act to be nice to them at all. Of course, Alan's Father was more abusive than all forty of these guys put together. He thought nothing of beating her for the slightest infractions of his rules like not bringing his morning paper in to him at exactly the time he wanted it each day. He'd whip off his leather belt and snap it several times across her bare arms, then tell her, "Be sure to wear a long-sleeved shirt to school today. You wouldn't want anyone to know how bad you've been." And her dear "loving" Stepmother wouldn't do anything but stand by waiting her turn to find some reason to berate her terribly. Naomi didn't know how she had the stamina and the courage to survive all those years without trying to fight back. Maybe it was just her unbridled stubbornness?

Before she could find anything to help her, she heard a rather loud knock at her door. An unfamiliar gray-haired woman apparently in her 60's was standing in the hall and nearly begged Naomi to let her in to talk.

"Hi, I'm Matilda Barlow."

"Hi."

"I'm Buddy's Mother. He was your daughter's 'main squeeze' as they'd say. Well...."

"So get on with whatever you have to tell me. Sad to say, I only remember your son as a smirking smart ass, if you can stand the unpainted truth," Naomi added angrily.

"Like your Lily he had his shortcomings."

"So why are you here, Matilda?"

"Oh, Naomi, this is very hard for me to share with you. I think Buddy is or I mean was your grandsons' Father."

"Hold on, your son wasn't even seeing my daughter the year before her sons were born. I hate to say it out loud but she had lots of men friends during that time who could have fathered her boys."

"No, Naomi, listen to me. My Buddy was stabbed in a street fight three weeks ago. Right before he died in the emergency room, he told me that Lily was convinced he was Tom and Ted's Father because they had a fling for old times' sake one weekend when she wasn't getting it on with anyone else or at least that's what she told him. The thing was she didn't want him around. He was so angry at her he cut off all contact though he did give her money that she drank or drugged away. Oh, Naomi, I had to tell you all of this, it was like my son's last wish for the truth to be known."

Overcome with this sad information, Naomi could only stare at the upset woman now sitting across from her. Why did Buddy wait all this time to tell his secret? She didn't understand. Why did some people do stuff like this to others? Why did her

Lovely Lily, her Flower never tell her or her boys what she knew? Was she that terribly angry about Buddy being her sons' Father? Why?

Then the probable reality hit her. Of course, in her crazed drunken and drugged state, she decided Buddy could never be a good Father so she denied him that right of ever knowing his sons or they him. Oh, the twists and turns of Fate!

Naomi got up and sat down beside Matilda on the sofa. She took her hand and held it. "Thank you, Matilda, for telling me all of this. I know it must have been very difficult for you to come here and admit this about your son and my daughter. If what you've told me is true, we're related and my grandsons have another Grandma."

"Should we tell them about this?"

"I don't know. Let me think about that. They've always wanted to know who their Father was. I did too of course. OK... here's what we'll do. I'd like you to come to dinner here tomorrow night. We'll tell them together. Sad, though, that they'll never meet Buddy, but you can tell them all about him."

"You are one remarkable woman, Naomi. No wonder Lily and Buddy's sons have turned out so well despite their parents' problems. Tom and Ted are a testament to you as a wonderful Grandmother."

"But how do you know about them?"

"Before I came here, I talked to some people who know

them at their school. They had nothing but wonderful things to say about them."

Another ten minutes passed as the two women exchanged stories and emotions. As Matilda stood up to leave, Naomi's blue-green eyes sparkled and she said, "Thank you again, Matilda. You don't know how good you've made me feel and I'm very sorry for the loss of your son."

"I appreciate that, Naomi. I better get going now and put something on the table for my Charlie."

"Oh, please bring him with you to dinner Friday at 7?"

The two Grandmothers embraced at the door of Naomi's apartment. As Matilda scrambled down the stairs, Naomi could almost feel the joy and relief in her step. She smiled then from ear to shining ear as she closed the door and began to think about what to make for the special dinner with Lily Larson, the Barlows and their grandsons.

Tom and Ted accepted the long overdue word about their Father and their Aunt Lily. They hugged their newly found family members and planned to meet again soon. When the guests left after a chicken dinner with apple pie for dessert, Naomi sat with her grandsons as both asked, "Why?" at the same time.

Naomi knew exactly what they meant, "Look, my dearest ones, when your Mother died, you were only nine years old. I just couldn't overwhelm you with all the ghastly details of her passing even all these years later. Please forgive me. As you know from the Barlows, I just found out about their son most likely being your Father. Actually just a few days ago when Buddy's Mother came here to tell me. Who can explain why people make the decisions they make? I'm very sorry for whatever pain I caused you two dear boys." At that Naomi reached out and pulled Tom and Ted into her arms. They were all at a new place now - a deeper, more loving place of acceptance and understanding.

The next morning, her weary bones and painful body causing an especially dramatic headache, she was getting ready for work dreading the day ahead. She could barely pour herself a cup of coffee her head was throbbing so hard. Those special memories from the previous night notwithstanding, Naomi kept looking in all of the cabinets in the apartment pulling out-of-date medications to throw away in the process. Searching, searching, searching throughout her modest home.

Then finally in the kitchen she spied a half empty bottle of whiskey pushed all the way back on one of the shelves behind containers of tea and sugar and flour. It passed her mind that it probably had been her Lovely Lily, her Flower's stash from years ago, but no matter. She couldn't let that bother her now. She just had to have something to dull the pain coursing through her body. How would she otherwise be able to stay on her feet taking care of all those men on the boat for hours?

She emptied the bottle into a tall glass, added a splash of water and drank all of it down in three gulps. "Hey ho. Hippy do! That done it so frigging fine!" she yelped. "Flying high now! Come on down, you crazy guys, this here dame's ready to deal with every frigging one of you now!"

Her body wavered back and forth as she tottered down the street to the bus stop. Very carefully, she managed to pull her tired bones up the three steps, which seemed like thirty to her. She sank down in a seat near the front next to a black woman in a green and pink dress who looked somehow familiar.

She soon became convinced this was the bartender from her Lovely Lily, her Flower's favorite pub. Oh how she hated going there to bring her drunk little girl home!

She glared at the woman with outright scorn. Unable to hold her rage in check, she asked, her voice slurring as she did, "Don't you remember me, lady? I'm the Mother of that lovely Flower named Lily you kept giving drinks to one night. Because of your booze, she fell and hit her head and bled to death! Bet you didn't know all that, you horrible excuse for a human being! How could you do that to my only child, my Lovely Lily, my Flower?"

As she continued to berate the stranger, Naomi's voice became increasingly strident, but the other woman remained quiet throughout her tirade. Caught as she was in the window seat, she could only squirm around uncomfortably like a prisoner being tortured by listening to this old woman's venomous condemnations. At first, the passengers in nearby seats turned to stare at the two women but then quickly returned to reading their newspapers or sipping their bitter coffees.

But Naomi wasn't finished yet. "Yes, indeed, you killed my only daughter with all your liquor. Your devil's water! You killed my Lovely Lily, my Flower, you wicked witch!"

At that she began pounding on the poor woman's arm although in her state it wasn't with much force. Still the stranger remained silent though she could feel her blood pressure rising and rising. She might have glared a "Get Away from Me, Lady!" at Naomi, but since she was a actually a nun wearing regular clothes, she simply prayed for the sad woman who had lost her daughter to drinking.

Naomi continued her tirade against her with, "Don't you have anything to say for yourself?"

At that the woman proclaimed, "To those who love God all things work together unto good."

Hearing that line from scripture, Naomi was caught so off guard that she tripped off the bus at the next stop without paying any attention to where she was. It took her a few minutes to orient herself before she realized she was stranded in a relatively run down area of the city that scared her right down to the varicose veins in her legs. She stood shaking and bewildered not knowing what to do or where to turn.

Inexplicably, the face of the old nun who was celebrating her ninety-fifth birthday on the boat suddenly flashed across her memory. No, Sister Eustacia would never be caught in a situation like this, damn it! She'd always be taken care of. She would never have to ride on a crowded bus or have to sit beside a woman who she thought caused her only daughter's death! Those nuns would always be driven wherever they had to go. How easy they lived with no problems! And even if they might have a few, they couldn't be really hard ones like all of hers. No way would they have to deal with working almost into their 80's to support two grandsons and help them get through graduate school. Or deal with the guilt of having their Mother, her Lovely Lily, her Flower, die because she couldn't get her to stop drinking and doing drugs and being with lots of men for money to buy booze.

No, those lucky nuns would never, ever be faced with problems like hers! Their lives were filled with prayer and care and good food and warm buildings and nice friends. They never had to worry about anything! She wondered if they had any idea of the major differences between their easy lives and her hard one. She could feel her face redden as she got angrier and angrier at the unfair tragedies Old Man Fate had sent her and cried out loud, "Oh Dearest God, why wouldn't you let me keep my Alan, the Love of my Life, and my Lovely Lily, my Flower? Why did you have to take both of them away from me? Why? Why?"

How jealous she was of all of those nuns and everything

they had. How they were always taken care of. How they never had to face a millionth of the problems she had to face in her life. It wasn't fair all they had compared to the little she had. In some part of her being she hated every one of those women especially that ninety-five year old one with the damn crooked headpiece enjoying a birthday bash on a luncheon cruise no less!

And to make matters worse for herself, she was now lost on this ominous street in a strange part of town. Alone. Like always. She stood in the middle of the debris covered sidewalk, not knowing what to do. After wandering aimlessly down a block, she eased her worn out body down on the curb and sobbed and sobbed wishing all her problems would just go away.

PART III

AIESHA
Coming Together

"Would you know my name
If I saw you in Heaven
Will it be the same
If I saw you in Heaven
I must be strong to carry on."

(Eric Clapton 1992)

Chapter 7

Depression Overcome

When Aiesha heard some traffic outside her apartment building, she peered out her bedroom window hoping to see her boyfriend Davon arriving. Instead she watched an old woman lumber down the steps of a bus like she was scared or really mad.

She looked familiar in some way. Rewinding her memory through the past few weeks, she scratched her head and zoned out for a moment. "Hold on," she thought to herself. This is strange. It was that wrinkled old lady waitress from the cruise on the harbor last week! What in the world was she doing here? Was she just lost or maybe something else was wrong, Big Time.

For a minute Aiesha didn't have a clue about what she should do about this woman. Then she looked out the window again and saw her standing in the middle of the sidewalk like she was stranded in the middle of the jungle and didn't know what to do next.

Aiesha decided she had to help the woman before anything preventable happened. She was reminded of her maternal Grandma Winnie she had only seen in old photos since she died before she was born. She was gray-haired and very wrinkled like the waitress from the boat. From what her Momma had told her, Grandma Winnie was easily frightened in any situation different from her every day world just like this woman from the boat seemed to be. One time her Mother told her about she even got disoriented on her own street, but she was nearly ninety at the time. Aiesha also recalled a recent conversation she had with her Mother about her Grandma.

"Oh, Honey, she was such a fun woman throughout most of her life. One time when she was going to be alone for a while at my sister's house when she wasn't feeling well, my sister called to check on her and she just told her, 'Oh, I'm fine here with two men under my bed!'"

"Wow, that must have really struck Aunt Lana as hilarious."

"Of course, it did. Your Grandma was such a good woman and supportive Mother. Whenever I had a big decision to make, she always said to me, 'Whatever will make you happy.' At first she wasn't too keen on your Daddy. She thought he was too forward and full of himself. Too eccentric and unconventional, so to say, for her perfect daughter."

"I'll tell you what, though, Aiesha. Your Grandma came to love your Daddy. In a short time he even became her favorite son-in-law. 'Whatever will make you happy,' she said and she realized that your Daddy did that for me."

"You really miss them, don't you, Momma?"

"Of course I do, Honey. It's been four years since your Father died in Iraq and twenty years since your Grandma passed on, but I feel they're still right here with me."

"I'm sorry I never got to know Grandma, but you know from what you just told me, I feel her in us. And I know Dad is here as well."

"Thank you, Honey. Such wonderful thoughts."

Flowing out of her reverie, Aiesha ran down the stairs of her building and out to the sidewalk, but the old woman wasn't there anymore! Where could she have gone to so fast? She peered up and down the street and noticed someone sitting on the curb a few buildings away. It had to be her.

When Aiesha sat down beside the old woman, she saw streams of tears flowing down every ridge of her wrinkled face discoloring her shirt.

She turned to the woman and asked, "Aren't you from that harbor cruise I was on the other week? What're you doing here?"

The old woman looked up at the young black girl beside

her and nodded. "I... I got off the bus at the wrong stop... I was so upset I didn't realize... I made a mistake... the woman wasn't... I...."

"Hey, that's OK. Let me help you up. Another bus will be by here in 30 minutes. My name is Aiesha. What's yours?"

"I'm Naomi," she muttered.

"So don't you work on the harbor cruise?"

"Yes, I do work there. Oh no! Oh no! I'm going to be late for work if I have to wait that long and then I'll get fired and I can't let that happen. A big group of golfing buddies is coming on the boat today. I have to get there as soon as I can. Oh, what am I going to do? My grandsons and I need every single dollar I can make." The old woman sobbed rubbing her eyes. Aiesha noticed they changed from brown to blue-green when she stopped crying and wiped her face with the sleeve of her jacket.

Aiesha didn't know how or if she could do anything to help this unfortunate woman. She sat thinking for a few minutes and then jumped up suddenly. "I know. I'll call my boyfriend Davon. He has a bike. I mean a motorcycle. Maybe he could get you to the boat on time."

"Oh, no, Honey, that's nice of you and I appreciate your offer, but I've never..."

Before Naomi could protest again, Aiesha had her cell phone out and was cooing to her boyfriend, "Yeah, Davon Honey, you'd do your good deed for the year if you'd do this for me. Then tonight we can go see that new flick you've been talking about, OK? I'll even treat you to a big bag of popcorn."

Ten minutes later when the teen pulled up and realized it was a white woman and an old one at that who was going to ride behind him, he almost tore off down the street without her, but Aiesha reminded him about his good deed and the movie and popcorn later. Then she carefully helped Naomi scramble on behind Davon. He sped off to the harbor with a roar of his bike.

Naomi was never so afraid in all her nearly eighty years! Without a helmet and halfway off the seat, she could almost feel her heart sink to her toes and her gray hair turn pure white, but after only a few minutes she became overwhelmed by the fun of the ride and let her head flow back into the wind as she laughed out loud. How exhilarated and alive she felt! During this most thrilling ride of her long life, all her problems, jealousies, anger and self pity simply blew away in the wind! No more concerns about her grandsons or guilt about how their Mother, her Lovely Lily, her Flower had died or jealousy about the easy life the old nun from the harbor cruise with her headpiece on crooked and her fellow sisters enjoyed.

When she uneasily slipped off the bike on the street near the boat, the world with all its problems gushed back to her with a power that almost knocked her down. With a wavering voice she thanked the tall motorcyclist and watched him disappear into the traffic before she climbed onto the boat. Tottering up the gangplank, she remembered a line from a popular song from ages ago which then played in her mind the whole afternoon. "Fun! Fun! Fun! Til Daddy takes the T-bird away!"

When Davon got back to Aiesha's, he was more than ready to go out with her. A star basketball player, he sped up the steps three at a time to her apartment. He knocked several times without getting an answer. Finally, Aiesha flung open the door and asked, "What took you so long, Hon?"

"What'ca mean, Sweets? I flew back here as fast as I could."

"Well, did you have a good time with that old lady or what?'

"No way, but she sure had one all time great time with me, though, hooting and hollering once we got going!"

"How could she not have fun sitting behind you, Davon?"

"You got that right, Isha! Now let's get going."

"Can't now, Hon. I have some chores to do and some studying. Let's go to the 7 o'clock."

"Well, what 'bout me in between time?"

"I'm sure you'll find something to do like write that big Hamlet essay for English due tomorrow."

"You know how I hate doin' that! What do I care about some guy who can't decide whether or not to get back at his uncle for killing his Father by dropping poison in his ear?"

Laughing, Aiesha answered, "See you round 'bout six-thirty. Bye."

Then she gave her friend a soft shove out the door just as her Momma called out, "Who was that, Aiesha? I hope it wasn't that basketball player friend of yours. Didn't you tell me you have a big math test coming up soon? You can't be taking any time out from your study to see that boy."

"But I have been studying for the test, Momma!"

"Well go back to your algebra book and forget about Davon at least for tonight!"

Aiesha spent the next few hours trying her best to review mind-bending mathematical equations, but she kept thinking about that waitress from her senior class' luncheon cruise who was lost in her neighborhood. She reminded her of someone she saw once when she was a little girl. Someone who really stood out in her memory for some reason. Yeah, someone who used to come to the bar where her Momma worked.

How Aiesha hated that dive! The place smelled of stale beer and man sweat and cigarette smoke and some other disgusting odor she couldn't identify. What really got her was how some of the guys there, mostly blacks, only a few whites, were always trying to touch her Momma. Trying to get her to pay attention to them. Whistling at her and calling her "Dearie" and "Darlin" and "Doll Baby." They were so sickening! Some even kissed her good bye before they staggered out of the place although only on the cheek. It would have much more repulsive if they had kissed her on the mouth! It bothered her a lot that her Momma never seemed to mind their lecherous attention at all. Was it part of a game she played to get their big tips and keep them coming back? She didn't know for sure, but she wanted to believe that was her plan. That was the only way she could bring herself to accept how those obnoxious men treated her.

Then there was that one utterly horrible night that she could never, ever forget! She was waiting for her Momma to get off work. She had to be at the bar because among other things, Aiesha's little sister was at a friend's sleep over and their neighbors were out of town. She didn't like staying in the apartment all by herself so she begged her Momma to let her tag along with her to work. She was being good reading a book at a table way back in the corner of the room when it all started. Thinking back, she wondered if her Momma had filled in the details of what she thought she remembered of that night....

A white woman was sitting at the bar talking loud to her Momma. "Come on, Maya. One more beer for the road! I'm so...."

"No, Lily. Enough's enough and you've had more than that now!"

"Listen to me, I'll tell you when to stop not the other way around!"

"Yeah, I hear you loud and clear, Lily, but I promised your Mother."

"What in the hell did you promise that old woman who's always on my case?"

"That I'd stop serving you before...."

"Before she said so? Tell me, you black..."

"Settle down, Lily. Come on, cool down nice and easy."

"Easy. Easy you say. Like when the sky turns purple! I have rights, you know. I'm a paying customer, damn it! You're my slave to do what I say. You don't have any other choice!"

"No way am I your slave or anyone else's. You're out of control Lily, so I'm cutting you off now and that's that!"

"Oh, no you're aren't, lady! I have the freakin' money and you have the freakin' beer... so come on...you owe me."

"What in the world could I possibly owe you, Lily?"

"For one thing I bring in a hell of a lot of business to this hole in the wall sorry excuse of a bar so you get some big tips from all the guys I know. Some of them are stinkin' rich."

"OK then why did that loser over there with your friend Maxie only give me a dollar tip for his forty dollar bar tab? You're trying my patience, Lily. I told you you're not getting any more drinks so go home to your two sons. They need you. You can't expect your Mother to be taking care of them all the time, poor woman. Now get out of here!"

"Stop sermonizing me, Maya. I'm a big girl. I sure as hell don't need some black woman tellin' me what to do or not to do, you hear! You're not my Mother, damn you!"

"And a good thing too. If I were, I'd...."

"You'd what?"

"I'd put you in your place, that's for sure. No more carousing. No more drinking and doing whatever else with a slew of men. That's what I'd do!"

"Well, la di da! And how would you keep me from doin' all that? Do you think you're my almighty great black Mother substitute now! Well, you make me sick, you know that!"

"Get a life, Lily. I told you you're out of control. Go home to your two little boys!"

"Didn't you hear me to tell you you're not my Mother! Stop your God damned yellin' at me and tellin' me what to do. And who are you anyway to talk when your little girl's sittin' over there in this bar, by damn, hanging out with us degenerates! At least my boys are safe at home and not here in this awful place. Now give me another freakin' beer right now, you God damned hypocrite!"

"Oh, OK. Stop badgering me! God help me, you win, Lily. Here's your last beer and then get out of here and don't come back!" Considering what happened before that fateful night ended, Maya would always regret what would become her last words to Lily.

Aiesha listened and watched her Momma trying to deal with the drunk white woman. She hoped she'd leave before she caused any trouble. Her Momma just couldn't lose her job. As young as she was then she knew her family needed the money, especially from the tips she brought home each night. She never wanted to have to go on Welfare again. Towards the end of the month all they ate for meals was peanut butter sandwiches without even any jelly on them and only drank water to wash them down. She never wanted to eat like that again. No, not ever!

All of a sudden Aiesha heard a loud shattering of glass. She looked up from her book and saw the drunk white lady throwing her mug across the bar hitting a line of bottles in front of the long mirror there. Fortunately, her Momma was waiting on some men down at the other end of the bar then so none of the pieces of glass cut her.

Next she saw the same white lady swing off her bar stool and almost fall flat on her face on the floor. When she ran over to help her up, the woman simply stared at her for a few seconds as her blue-green eyes turned brown and then pushed her aside roughly and tottered out of the bar. Though she never saw her again, she did see similar changing eyes some other time and place. Only she didn't remember where or when right away....

Yes, there was something about that woman her Momma called Lily. She reminded Aiesha of someone she had seen recently. But who? Who? Of course, that waitress she got Davon to ride to work today on his motorcycle! What was it about the two of them that connected them in her mind? Something about their eyes? Yeah, how they changed colors from blue-green to brown or were they sometimes blue-green then brown? She had seen that happen even in the few minutes she was up close to that drunk white lady that one night in the bar. She had never forgotten how strange they seemed. And last week on that luncheon boat, that wrinkled old waitress' eyes had changed from blue-green to brown too! But so what?

Then she remembered something from a recent bio class on genetics. What was the connection? She pulled out her notes and started scanning them for relevant data. She found one rather important section with information from a website called AllAboutVision.com.

They learned that eye color is a trait that's inherited and caused by more than one gene. Blue eyes come from a small amount of melanin which protects from sun damage; green from a larger amount and brown from melanin-rich irises. "Wait!" she said to herself, "There's another piece of info on the same subject that's very important."

Finding a particularly highlighted part of her notes, she was taken aback. When the pupil size changes, the eye color can appear to change because the pigments in the iris spread apart. Stress and powerful emotions can alter the iris color and the pupil size, thus making the eyes change colors!

All of this was very interesting stuff for Aiesha to recall, but right now she knew she had to focus on her algebra review. She became so immersed in it that she hardly realized when she was finally all alone in the apartment. She wondered where Davon was. It was 6:30 already. Almost at the same moment she heard an ambulance scream down on the street outside the apartment building, her cell phone rang. Flicking it on quickly, she asked, "What's up?"

"Isha, Tyrell here. I'm really hating to tell you this but..."

"What, Tyrell? What is it? I'm waiting for Davon to come over. Matter of fact, he may be trying to call me right now so...."

"No, he won't. I mean he can't."

"What are you trying to tell me, Tyrell?"

"It's about Davon, Isha. He's hurt. He's...."

"What happened? Just tell me, Tyrell!"

"In the wrong place at the wrong time. A guy with a gun."

"Where is he? Is he OK?" Aiesha asked, nearly hysterical.

"Try to calm down, Isha. Got shot up pretty bad. He's in Mercy's ER."

"Oh, Tyrell, can you get your Father's car and take me there? Please!"

"Yeah, I'll be over at your place as soon as I can."

"Hurry, Tyrell. I'll be outside."

Less than twenty minutes later the two teens ran into the emergency room at Mercy. Davon's parents were standing in the waiting room literally crying on each other's shoulders. "Gone!" was the only world Aiesha could make out before she collapsed on the floor. Tyrell tried to comfort her when he pulled her up, but she just pushed him away hugging herself for solace. She didn't know how long they stayed in the waiting room. Later she only remembered embracing her boyfriend's parents and saying how sorry she was before Tyrell carried her to his Father's car and drove her home.

That night she finally fell asleep but only after hours of tossing and turning.

Inexplicably, she found herself at the scene of a murder. She was standing on the corner of an unknown street in the arms of Tyrell, of all people, when she heard Davon scream. She told Tyrell, "Sweets, it's nothing. Let's go to my place. I have to get out of here." Was it really Davon's moaning getting softer and softer that she heard as she and Tyrell hurried away down the street together?

Aiesha woke in a panic, her nightmare as real as the morning sun now shining in through her window. She didn't know what to make of it. She wasn't "into" Tyrell that way. Davon was her Main Squeeze. She blamed herself for how he died. Wasn't it her fault she had put him off until the evening which meant he was out there on the street somewhere on the way when....

She flew to the bathroom making it just in time to throw up in the commode and then collapse on the floor moaning over and over, "Why? Why?" Her Mother found her there asleep with her head on the rug, her body curled up in a fetal position. She had a hard time rousing her, but when she did, Aiesha continued moaning, "Why? Why?"

At his gravesite Aiesha kept seeing Davon play Center on the school's basketball team as she cheered him on. Then the big celebration after each win. Dinner every week at his house. At his wake his Mother told Aiesha one thing she would never forget, "Our Davon's in Heaven with his Granddad and Grandma he loved a lot. They're watching over you and all of us."

Still weeks later Aiesha couldn't shake her grief. No one in her family could reach her, not even her Mother. She cried her eyes scarlet and swollen. She slept fitfully for only an hour or two each night. She kept hearing herself promise Davon, "I'll see you later."

"Later" became like a gigantic winged cockroach crawling all over her body as though it was telling her repeatedly, "If only you hadn't.... If only you hadn't...." Feeling like she'd die herself of guilt, she sank deeper into the throes of depression as the days tiptoed by.

Even Davon's Mother couldn't really soothe her, not that she didn't try. An extremely religious and caring woman, she sent Aiesha a page with several Psalms she had copied in her unique calligraphy:

"May the Lord answer you in your day of trouble;

May the name of the God of Jacob defend you;

May He send you help from the sanctuary,

And strengthen you out of Zion." Psalm 20: 1-2

"Yes, though I walk through the valley of

the shadow of death,

I will fear no evil;

For you are with me." Psalm 23:4

"Oh give thanks to the God of Heaven for his mercy endures forever." Psalm 136:26

To some degree Aiesha felt solace from these quotes but not enough to pull her out of her depression. It seemed like no one and nothing could do that.

One evening the next week her friend Tyrell dropped by her apartment to check on her. He took one look at her rumbled clothes, pale drawn face and bloodshot eyes and knew she was in big trouble. "Oh, Isha, let me get you out of the house for awhile. We can take a walk, go to the mall or get a sundae down at Francie's. Anything you want to do."

Her red eyes tearing up, Aiesha simply nodded her head "No" and waved him out the door. She knew he meant well, but she just couldn't be around him. He reminded her too much of Davon. Her Davon now gone! Gone! She ran up the stairs crying her eyes out, it seemed to her, for the hundredth time that day.

That night because she couldn't get to sleep again no matter how hard she tried, she sat up in bed writing in her journal. "I don't know what to do about Tyrell. We've been friends along with Davon for almost all our lives. We used to call ourselves The Three Black Musketeers. I'm thinking now that Tyrell was never happy I picked Davon to be my Main Man when we became teenagers. Yeah, my sense is he's probably still not happy now that I keep pushing him away. But it was my choice to make about who I wanted to be with. Not anyone else's! I'm my Own Person or I'm nothing! So I'll just have to deal with Tyrell as best I can. He's been so nice to me since Davon, but.... but.... he.... can't be.... Oh, I can't write anymore tonight."

When Aiesha finally fell into a restless sleep, her previous nightmare at Davon's murder scene with Tyrell haunted her throughout the night.

Weeks passed as she continued being stuck in a quagmire of depression, refusing to let anyone help her. Her Mother became so worried about her that she called the school counselor to ask for help. Aiesha got word during her history class to report to the counselor's office.

"Hi, Ms. Earle."

"Good morning, Aiesha. I'm glad you came in."

"So what's happening? Why'd you get me out of class?"

"I wanted to touch base with you to see how you're doing, Aiesha."

"Oh, I'm Great! Marvelous actually," she answered without honesty.

At this response, Ms. Earle's stared at her knowingly. She was well aware of this denial technique so many teenagers used. And many adults for that matter as well.

Then Aiesha opened up like a pot of popcorn still popping with the lid off. What she said sounded like one extended sentence because she hardly took even one breath throughout the whole explanation. "OK, OK, Mrs. Earle so I'm actually feeling terrible! Like the earth sucked Davon into a huge hole and I couldn't do nothing to save him so here I am all alone. I just can't get over it! It happened so fast. I saw him that afternoon. He gave a ride on his motorcycle as a favor to someone I kind of knew. And he was coming over that night to go to a movie with me. As a matter of fact, he was probably on his way when...."

The lone word "Gone!" from the hospital hit her again and Aiesha broke down sobbing long and hard. Her counselor kept passing her tissue after tissue for the next fifteen minutes. Then Aiesha blew her nose and tried to apologize, "Oh, Ms. Earle, I... I'm so... sor...."

"No, you don't have to say anything, Aiesha. I lost a very good friend too when I was just a few years older than you are. I cried a lot for a long time afterwards. So as much as anyone can,

I kind of understand what you're going through."

"Thanks for putting it that way, Ms. Earle. The thing is no one can really get how I feel. No one can completely understand me. No one in my family even my Momma or my other really good friend from forever Tyrell. Did you know that he and Davon and I used to call ourselves The Three Black Musketeers?"

"But, Aiesha, you don't have to be this way...."

"I know what you're going to say, Ms. Earle. It's my own problem, right? I'm the only one who can get me out of this. I have to help myself feel better because no one else can."

"Yes, Aiesha. That's pretty much the same awareness I eventually came to myself many years ago. Somehow, no matter how hard it is, you do have to find a way to get beyond this. Other people who mean well like your Mother or your good friend Tyrell can try to help you, but ultimately you have to find a way to help yourself. And that's what's so extremely difficult. I know I had to face that myself more than once so far in my life."

"So what did you do to move on, to help yourself when your friend died, Ms. Earle?"

"Let's see, I remember first I became a volunteer at a local hospital visiting patients in the eye surgery and cancer wards. Talking to them really got my mind off my own problems at least for a little while. Oh, yes, I also joined a dancing group and went out dancing several nights a week. I put in a lot of extra hours at work too."

"I don't know about the dancing but..."

"Wait a minute, Aiesha. I have an idea. A friend of mine from graduate school, who's now the administrator of a nursing home several miles from here, called me yesterday wondering if any students needed community service hours because she's in desperate need of any help she can get. Just the other day one of her key staff had an unexpected C-section, but her replacement can't start for a few weeks. Maybe you can volunteer to help her in the meantime."

"Oh, I don't know, Ms. Earle. I really don't have any experience to do that."

"Well, my friend said she'd be happy with someone who would simply befriend the old nuns especially one who's descending more and more into Alzheimer's every day. Maybe you could help her out in any way you can but mostly by listening to her."

"Yeah, maybe. I'll think about it, OK, Ms. Earle?"

"All right, Aiesha, but my friend needs someone right away. Could you please tell me your answer tomorrow morning? I'd really appreciate it and I know my friend would too."

"Sure. I'll let you know before first period. I'm off to math now. Big test. Bye."

For some reason she couldn't figure out, Aiesha started to feel better almost as soon as she left her counselor's office so much so that by the end of her last class that afternoon, she dropped by Ms. Earle's office and told her she would do the volunteer work at the retirement home.

That night Aiesha wrote in her journal, "I don't understand why I started feeling better after talking to my counselor. I guess it was because she seemed to understand me so I'm going to take her up on volunteering at Saint Clara's Retirement Home. Maybe going there will get my mind off what happened to Davon at least for a little while. I miss him so much! He was one person who really and truly got me! He knew what made me tick and knew where I was coming from. I just don't understand. Why did he have to die the senseless way he did? Momma told me that our minister said we can't understand God's plans for us or why things happen the way they do. Especially bad things. He's certainly right about that. I don't know if I'll ever get why this happened to Davon. Oh why did he have to leave me? I can't believe he's really gone. I suppose everyone who's lost someone special feels the same way."

When she finally fell asleep, for once in a long time she had a lovely dream.

She and Davon were standing in line waiting to ride a new very scary roller coaster at an amazing amusement park. He held her hand tightly as they scrambled onto the ride and he assured her, "I'll always be right here with you, Isha. Don't ever forget that!" They embraced and she cried in his arms. Feeling so secure and loved, Aiesha realized the ride began moving up the ramp towards the heavens. As it accelerated into twists and turns, she and Davon flew off arm in arm into the deep blue sky!

Aiesha woke with a wide smile on her face wanting with her whole heart and soul to believe she and Davon had actually flown into the sky together, but knowing he would always be "there" for her in her memory. That awareness made her feel able to go on with her life without him... somehow.

The next Sunday afternoon she walked up to the front desk at Saint Clara's Retirement Home for the first time. She was assigned to a nun named Sister Eustacia, the one Ms. Earle said had Alzheimer's. As soon as she opened the door to her room, Aiesha realized this nun seemed familiar. Where in the world had she seen her before? She hardly ever went anywhere nuns would be, particularly old lady nuns like this one with her headpiece on crooked.

Then it hit her! She was the nun who had smiled at her several times for some reason during her senior class' luncheon cruise several weeks ago. That old lady nun who kept shaking her head like it wasn't on tight. The one celebrating her ninety something birthday!

What a coincidence! As soon as that reaction registered in her brain, Aiesha remembered she didn't believe in "coincidences." No, this was a meaningful event. She was convinced that she'd been sent to get to know this nun and help her in some way. For some even stranger reason she sensed this old nun was even going to help her too somehow.

"Hi, Sister Eustacia. My name's Aiesha. I'm going to be visiting you whenever I can in the next few weeks and months."

"OK, dear. Come and sit down. Mother told me the ship's about to pull out from the shore soon and move into the Atlantic. Or is it the Pacific? Oh what fun we're going to have! I'm sure James will find an escort for you, and then we'll all dance the Charleston together. What a great time we'll have! Oh and wouldn't you like a Flapper dress to wear too? I'm sure James' sister will have another one to lend to you. By the way, did you know I watched you and your boyfriend dancing this afternoon at lunch on the boat?"

"Oh, that would have been Davon. Oh Sister, it was on the harbor cruise the last time we danced together."

"So what happened to him? Did your Father forbid you to see him?"

"No, Sister. Oh it's so hard to say this. He was in the wrong place at the wrong time and killed by a bullet."

"Oh, my dear, I'm so sorry! I've lost someone special too. Oh, but I have to tell you this, you and your boyfriend were dancing so close together in such a way Father would never have approved of. Oh, he'd be so infuriated if he saw me doing that with James!"

"Are you talking about your real Father, Sister?"

"Oh, yes. Extremely strict. Very religious. No fun and games otherwise horrible punishments. How he hated James! He even threatened to kill him, would you believe? I was so scared for him! Maybe you know what happened to him. I have to find him. I miss him so much!"

Aiesha watched in horror as the old nun's body almost went into convulsions for a few moments. She thought she might be reliving a bad experience because her disjointed and painful memories continued.

"Everyone thought it was so sad except me. Losing all his money. Jumping eighteen floors to the ground. His blood and insides all over the street. Then Mother said 'stay a good nun' and left me forever too. Been doing penance all these years for my sins. All kinds of penance... kneeling for long times in the chapel... praying with my arms outstretched in my room... fasting even before I was twenty-one. But oh, all the time missing James. Have you seen him? Oh, where can he be?"

Aiesha was embarrassed listening and trying to fill in the gaps of what Sister Eustacia said. Was it her Father who supposedly had lost all his money in the stock market crash of '29 she read about in history class? Did he really jump from the eighteenth floor of some building onto the street? And what sort of things could this old woman have done in her life to still be doing so much penance for all these years? Didn't someone on the luncheon cruise say she'd been a nun for eight decades! Longer than most people lived.

She felt tears welling up in her eyes now as she thought about Davon again. This old nun has lived nearly eighty more years so far, more than four times as many as he got. Then she looked over at Sister whose blue-green eyes changed to brown and were welling up too as she kept chanting "James" over and over again. Where was this James and why was Sister so intent on finding him? How could she help this confused old woman deal with her pain?

Something pulled at her from behind the doors of her memory. Another person with changing eyes, blue-green and brown. A woman called Lily. No, it couldn't be that one she was remembering earlier from her Mother's bar. How in the world could it possibly be the same person? She decided she'd still try to learn more from talking to Sister Eustacia even though she knew her mind wasn't all there and her memory was rather skewed.

"Sister Eustacia, did you ever know a woman named Lily? Was she a relative or maybe a friend of yours?"

"No. No one named Lily. I never got to name our little one. Gone. Taken away. Told she had died but I couldn't believe it. James didn't know about her. Never got to tell him before he left his house. Oh, our little one! Gone. Lost. Dead. Given away. Can you help me?"

"But who was James, Sister? And the little one?"

"I can't say anything more. No! No! No! I promised. No one can know! Not Father. Not Mother. Not even any of the other sisters. No one was to know where I went, what was going to happen there. I had to keep quiet. Do my studies. No visitors. No talking after the Grand Silence. Praying with arms outstretched. Kneeling extra hours in chapel. Three vows. Be poor. Stay pure. Always follow someone else's orders. No crying over the past now. But do you know what happened to my James? I've been looking for him for a long time. No one seems to know where he went. Do you know? I have to tell him about our...."

Aiesha was taken aback and overwhelmed at what she had just heard the old nun say. What could she tell her? She tried her best. "I'm sorry, Sister, but I don't know who James is or where he is. When and where did you see him last?"

"Let me think. Oh, yes, the summer of '28 in a hotel lobby in Paris. Oh, how I miss him every day! Have you seen him anywhere around here? I've been looking all over for him. I have to tell him about our little...."

"What do you want to tell James?"

"No, I can't tell you! Only him if I knew where he was... if you could tell me. Dear Mother Elias told me not to tell anyone. Not even my parents! Oh, no! Oh, no! I must talk to James. Do you know where I can find him? Please tell me. I must see him."

"Unfortunately, I don't know where he is, Sister. I'm so sorry. Why can't you tell anyone but him whatever it is about your little...."

"Mother Elias said not to. Not even Father and Mother. But I so wanted to tell James but Father wouldn't let me see him. Locked me in my room... Then I had to go all alone to that place. No letters. No visitors. So lonely. So very lonely. Never told anyone about... wicked priest... what he tried to do... Not even Mother Elias... Oh, I'm so, so weary. Tired. Can't talk any...."

Sister's whole being seemed to dissolve into a tall glass of tears. Her body slumped into the chair. Her breathing became quite labored. Aiesha put her arms around her and softly crooned, "I'm so sad, Sister, for whatever it is you can't tell anyone. Would you like me to help you get into bed now so you can rest?"

"Rest? I haven't had any rest, real rest, since.... I don't remem...."

"Come on now, Sister. Here let me help you take off your shoes."

"No, James, I can't take anything off! Father would not approve of it! He'd be very so angry at us! He'll punish me worse than the last time! I can't.... No, I can't! No! No!"

Aiesha really didn't know what to do next. She was more dumbfounded than ever. She couldn't get the old nun to budge out of her wheelchair or let her help take off her dowdy black shoes. She kept insisting, "I can't take them off, James! No, don't touch my hair! I can't put that tight dress on! No... Don't... Don't go there! No, don't touch me there! Oh, how different everything would've... if I'd just... would I be here... like this... without anyone?"

The old nun's head began sinking down onto her chest now as she started to snore lightly. All Aiesha could think was that she had worn herself out remembering whatever it was that any listener would probably never understand. She looked out in the hall and motioned to an aide to come and take care of her. Then she patted the dozing nun's gnarled hands and started to leave the building.

Before she got to the front entrance, the aide caught up with Naomi anxious to convey a disconcerting experience Sister had recently.

The aide took Aiesha around the corner to an empty room so they could talk in private. "I've been working here for a few years, and she frequently talks about this James and wants to know where he is."

"Do you think he is an actual person?" queried Aiesha.

"Well, when I talked to the director of the Retirement Home about this James and should we try to find him, she told me the story of how Sister Eustacia ended up here."

Aiesha got the shivers as if she knew she was going to learn something important.

"When Sister was still living with the other nuns somewhere across town, this James person apparently visited her.

"He was an elderly white-haired man who walked with a cane. Sister became so agitated and distraught when he told her his name was James Sheppard that she screamed, 'Go away! There's no way you can be my James!' The hapless man left reluctantly. He had a big tear running down his white bearded face as he dolefully left. Then only about a week later, the same man's Obituary was in the local paper. There was no point in telling Sister since she was so disturbed when he had come to see her."

"Who knows if he was really the same person, but Sister Eustacia started to descend into dementia after he left, rambling about some seemingly fictional past. It got so bad that they couldn't deal with her and she had to be moved here under professional supervision. It has been about fifteen years we've been taking care of her at Saint Clara's. As time went by, she slowly stopped raving about James and would just sit and stare out the window. But after coming back from her birthday cruise, she really has been losing her mind moaning about James and her baby. We're really worried for her and we can't bring her back to reality."

"Wow, I appreciate you telling me all this," Aiesha said. "I came here because I think I may have found someone who knows her and can help bring back her memories."

"I hope you do because Sister is really not doing well."

"Unfortunately, I agree with you. Thank you so much for your help. See you next week." At this point, the two went their separate ways.

On her way home from Saint Clara's, Aiesha couldn't get the mysteries of Sister Eustacia's life out of her mind.

Chapter 8

Synchronicity Acknowledged

As the bus lumbered on its way through the city, Aiesha decided there was something she could do right away to begin to solve this puzzle. She could talk to that waitress from the luncheon cruise. When she realized the bus stopped within a few blocks of The Harbor Place where the boat was docked, she jumped off hoping she'd be able to see the woman before the afternoon voyage departed.

A bearded maintenance man told her that Naomi had unfortunately fallen down the stairs the day before and was now recuperating at home in bed. "No surprise," Aiesha said to herself. "She barely could get around, stumbling like she was in pain." The man wouldn't give out her telephone number or address no matter how much she begged him. He did happen to mention her last name, though. On her way to the phone book

189

Aiesha thought, "How many Naomi Renalt's could there be in the phone book?"

She was so excited when she hit pay dirt, finding the number almost right away and dialing it on her cell phone.

"Hello."

"Hi, I'm trying to reach a woman named Naomi who works on a luncheon cruise ship on the Baltimore harbor. Is she there?"

"Who's calling?"

"Someone from the luncheon cruise. My name's Aiesha. Look, I really would like to talk to Naomi. Would you please put her on the line?"

"She's my Grandmother, OK. Let me see if she's awake. She had a bad fall on that boat yesterday so her doctor gave her some strong meds."

"Thanks."

"Yeah. Just a minute."

It seemed much longer than a minute to Aiesha as she stood holding her cell phone to her ear waiting. Lots of people, probably mostly tourists, were milling around her. She found a seat on a curb apart from the crowds as she continued waiting. Finally, after what seemed like a very long time, she heard Tom's voice again.

"Well, my Grandmother's up now but I have to warn you, she's not feeling well. Please don't talk to her too long, Aiesha."

"Thanks. I'm on my cell phone and don't want it to run down before we talk."

Aiesha could barely hear the woman's raspy voice when she finally got on the line. "Hi, who's this?"

"I'm Aiesha from that group of teenagers on the luncheon cruise last week."

"I'm sorry. I don't remember meeting any of you kids."

"You're right, you probably didn't, Naomi."

"So how'd you get my name and number? What is this all about? I'm so damn tired you'll have to get to whatever it is you want from me quickly!"

"I'll get right to the point. I've been wondering about your peculiar eyes ever since that afternoon."

"What? Why in the world are you wondering about my eyes of all things? Look, I don't have time for this craziness or whatever it is you want!"

Aiesha could tell by Naomi's perturbed voice that she'd better try to get some fast answers from her before she hung up. "Maybe you remember that elderly nun who was celebrating her birthday that day."

"How could I forget her? Can you believe it? Someone living over nine decades!"

"Well, I just started volunteering at her retirement home and was assigned to her."

"So... what's that have to do with me?" Naomi barked

even though she was becoming more and more interested in this conversation. Sister Eustacia had been an important rock in her life. Although she was bitter, she had lost her like Alan and her Lily, now she felt like something momentous was about to happen.

"There's something about her and you and a woman who used to come into the bar where my Mother worked... a woman named Lily. All three of you have strange changing eyes from blue-green to brown and vice-versa."

Naomi couldn't respond for several minutes. It was as though this stranger put her hands through the phone and squeezed all the air out of her lungs! How could this young girl know her Lovely Lily, her Flower? Some words from an old song rang through her memory, "a free and gentle flower growing wild." That was her Lily. But what did this girl on the phone want? Why did that old nun and her imaginary friend named James mean anything to her? Naomi was confounded, scared and surprisingly even a bit excited though she couldn't understand why.

"Oh, come on, get to your point. What do you want from me? What's all this nonsense about people's eyes changing colors?" Naomi was less than polite because among other things she was stressed, tired and in pain. She wished she could've been nicer but her nerves were frazzled to the edges.

"Naomi, is there any way Sister and you and a woman

named Lily could be connected or related? And also do you know anything about a man named James?"

Aiesha could hear the old lady crying now. Sensing her sobs were coming from some place of long ago sad memories, she almost felt her pain across the telephone waves.

"Naomi, are you OK? Are you still there?"

"Yes, I...I am...only...."

"Are you up to keep on talking?"

"I...I don't...know."

"Naomi, maybe this isn't a good time. Maybe I should...."

"No. No. Stay on the line. Just give me a moment."

For at least ten minutes by her watch, Aiesha continued sitting on the curb waiting for Naomi to pull herself together. She watched a crowded water taxi glide across the harbor as she tried to imagine a way that Sister Eustacia and a man named James and Naomi and Lily could possibly be connected. It was a certainly a mystery, one she was absolutely determined to solve.

Suddenly, she heard a deep voice in her ear, "Hello, Tom here again. Apparently, the side effects of her meds are really taking a toll on her. My Grandmother can't talk to you anymore."

"But...."

"I'm sorry, but she can't talk so I'm hanging up now. Good bye."

Before Aiesha could respond, the line went dead. She sat shaking her head in the warm afternoon sun.

Were Naomi and Lily actually connected in some odd way? Do their changing eye colors really link them? She had to find out one way or another.

What she couldn't have known then was that Naomi really did want to continue their conversation. It was her grandson who couldn't stand to see her so distraught and decided enough was enough. His Grandmother wasn't up to dealing with whatever the girl on the phone had said to her. He always knew when she was really out of sorts emotionally and as a result was quite protective of her.

"Grandma, why don't you take a vacation day off from work? You are on the verge of collapsing. I'm worried about you and so is Ted."

"No, Tommy, I can't afford to take any time off. Our money's too tight right now. And besides I'm on the mend. Just a bit more rest and I'll be up and running 100% again."

"Who do you think you're fooling, Grandma? I wish you'd just give it up and quit that crazy job. We'll get by somehow. You don't have to kill yourself continuing to work so hard. Ted and I can find better jobs."

"Listen, Tom, I appreciate all your concern, really I do, but I have to keep on keeping on. I'll be fine. It keeps me going still being out there making my way in the world. I can't see myself lounging around all day just watching TV. I'd become a big wrinkled up vegetable. Is that what you'd want your dear

Grandma to become?"

The two laughed then in each other's arms, Tom knowing he'd lost the battle but feeling better letting his Grandma know how concerned he was about her well being. Their short conversation filled Naomi's heart with even more love for her Lovely Lily, her Flower's two adorable sons. She'd hang in there for them no matter what. It was the least she could do to honor their Mother's memory.

Aiesha's intuition was strong and nearly always right. Though she couldn't have known for sure, her best instincts insisted, "No, don't believe that guy. Find a way to talk to Naomi again. There's something else going on here. Much more than just a series of unconnected random coincidences."

She remembered learning in her Advanced Psychology II class about synchronicity or meaningful coincidences, ones that were intended to flow together into some series of messages. She pulled out her notebook from her oversized backpack and reread her sprawling handwriting:

Synchronicity - meaningful coincidences of seemingly improbable events...

Events at first considered random coincidences later found to be causally related... the world is intricately and holistically more organized than we can imagine...

An order of meaning transcending our human perspective...

Cosmic ordering... synchronicity used by the cosmos to guide people to change their actions for their benefit or unknown reasons...

If you expect the unexpected, synchronicity emerges... knowing something but not knowing how you know it....

Looking up, she heard her Momma come into the room and greet her. "Hi, Honey. What have you been up to today?" She was home from the same bar she had been working at all these years except now she was the Manager.

"Just reading my notes on synchronicity and playing Nancy Drew for a while, Momma."

"Synchronicity and Nancy Drew? What are you talking about?"

"Well, remember you told me you read that whole series when you were young. The ones about the really inquisitive teenager girl who solves lots of mysteries."

"Oh yes, but how are you acting like that Nancy Drew character, Aiesha?"

"Remember that night a really long time ago when I went with you to the bar because I was afraid to stay at home all by myself? I heard this woman you called Lily hassle you for more beer and then she threw her mug across the bar and...."

"Oh yes, how could I ever forget that night and what happened afterwards! That woman got real mad because I refused to serve her any more drinks. Her Mother...."

"Yeah, you told her that you promised her you wouldn't...."

"Sure. But she...."

"Momma, I think I might have just met that woman's Mother."

"How could you possibly know that?"

"Well, remember that luncheon cruise my senior class went on several weeks ago? There was this wrinkled old lady waitress hobbling around serving us. Something about her eyes - the way they turned from blue-green to brown made me think about that woman named Lily at your bar. When she fell that night because she was so drunk, I tried to help her up and she stared at me with that same kind of changing eyes I will never forget."

"Why are you telling me all this, Aiesha? It brings back such bad memories especially about finding out later how that alcoholic woman died. Apparently she fell and hit her head on a radiator and bled to death in her apartment building. I can't imagine how her Mother dealt with finding her like that. And I was the one who served her those last drinks that put her over the edge. I've always felt so guilty about that! In fact, I've had recurrent nightmares about that night for years. The worst one was....

I'm standing on top of the bar saying No. No. No! I look around the room but only see what looks like a lily partially crushed on the floor swimming in beer. All at once it moves as though it wants to tell me something. Only I can't hear!....

Every time I have this dream, I scream and wake up sweating scared out of my wits!"

"Oh, Momma, I didn't know about that. How awful!"

"Well, it gets worse as far as what actually happened that night. After that poor girl Lily threw up all over the bar, I was so intent on cleaning it up so people wouldn't leave that I lost track of what happened to her. As far as I know, she apparently left by herself and somehow managed to get home. My bouncer had suddenly gotten sick that night thanks to the old flu bug, so he could not have taken care of her. It was all my fault she left with no one to help her. I keep beating myself up for reneging on my promise to her Mother that I would curtail her alcohol. Oh, I've always felt so bad about what happened to her in the end! I've never forgiven myself for my part in it."

"But, Momma, how could you have known all of that would go down that way?"

"Well, of course, I couldn't have but still...."

"Why didn't you tell me all of this back then?"

"Oh, you were too young at that time, Honey. I decided it was best you didn't know all the details."

"I guess that makes sense, Momma, but let me tell you what else is really weird. There was this group of really old nuns on that cruise I went on with my class. One of them was celebrating her ninety-fifth birthday. Something about her made me smile at her a couple of times during the afternoon. Maybe it was the odd way she looked with her headpiece on crooked. I don't know, but she even smiled back at me though most of the time she really seemed somewhere else. In fact, her aide said this old nun never seemed sure where she was...."

"So?"

"Remember I told you the other day that my counselor asked me to volunteer at that retirement home across town called Saint Clara's?"

"That nun lives there, right?"

"Not only that. I was actually assigned to her and, believe it or not, at one point when I could really see her eyes, she was muttering about how her Father was so angry with her and they turned from...."

"Blue-green to brown. Oh that was just a big coincidence, Aiesha Honey."

"No, Momma, everything in me says there's some connection between her and that drunk lady Lily you're so guilty about and I have to find it somehow. So I need your help."

"I know that intuition of yours is almost always right on. Still I don't know...."

Maya had a flash of her Aiesha as a little girl of six. Even then she was telling and writing stories. Also, sensing things before they happened like when her favorite kitty lil' Softy got sick and was going to stop breathing. She always had a mind of her own knowing exactly what she wanted when she wanted it. Once when she was only four, her friend asked her if she'd like some ice cream. She told her loud and clear, "Only if it's strawberry!" The strangest thing she remembered from her earliest years was that she would tell people, even her Mother, what was bothering them if they seemed sad or angry. She could put two and two together so easily and tell us what we should or shouldn't do. Early on she even understood what a coincidence was or wasn't.

"Momma, you OK?" Aiesha saw her daydreaming and knew she was reminiscing.

"I'm fine. What were you saying, Honey?"

"Well, here's the thing. I just talked on the phone to Naomi Renalt, the waitress from the cruise. I think she could be Lily's Mother."

"Also I think there's a chance those two are related somehow to that old nun I'm helping to take care of at Saint Clara's. The one who celebrated her ninety-fifth birthday on the boat who smiled at me and I smiled back."

"Oh, come on now, Aiesha! Even you must know how strange that would be. How could...."

"But, Momma, truth is always stranger than fiction, isn't it?"

"How many times have you told me one of your favorite English teachers always says that? OK, so what is it you want me to do?"

"Would you please come with me to visit Naomi in person? Maybe she'll remember you and help us solve...."

"Now, wait just a minute, Aiesha. Don't you think this is going too far?"

"Maybe but I really feel Naomi and Sister Eustacia are..."

"No! You don't mean...."

"Yes, Mother and daughter."

"This would be too incredible and amazing, Honey?"

"Yes, Momma, it would be amazing but I suspect it now more than anything after talking to you."

"But why? You have so little to go on. Only eyes changing colors. Anyone would have to admit that's not much. Come on, 'get real' as they say."

"But, Momma, my instinct tells me there's so much more to...."

"All right if there's any way to somehow prove this connection, then what?"

"I'm not sure right now, Momma, but I'm convinced

Naomi would like to know if that old nun is really her Mother and Sister would like to know her daughter too, that is if she could stay lucid long enough to understand."

"What do you mean?"

"Well, Sister's almost a hundred and sometimes she isn't well, all there if you know what I mean. What I'm trying to say is sometimes she's more somewhere in the past than here and now."

"What's that disease called? Alzheimer's, isn't it? Do you think she has it, Honey?"

"Yeah, probably. I looked up on the Internet. Sister has all the symptoms. She repeats things over and over; she's obviously in and out of reality always talking about some guy named James; being afraid of her Father; ranting about her little one; she has huge mood swings; she's calm one minute and nearly hysterical the next. In fact, she mixed up the luncheon cruise boat on the Baltimore Harbor a few weeks ago, the one my class was on, with one she apparently sailed on the Atlantic Ocean a very long time ago. Also, I noticed that she must have had at least four layers of clothes on in what I thought was a very warm building. Over top of her rumpled habit, she was wearing three sweaters of various colors and a long wool shawl over them. Oh yes, she mentioned having a secret, apparently from a long time ago, that she wasn't allowed to tell anyone. And she especially seemed to have an obsession with her Father not approving of a lot of things."

"So you think these are all indications of Alzheimer's, Aiesha?"

"Yes but the problem is I don't know if Sister in her current out-of-touch-with-reality condition would understand even if her supposed daughter was still alive. But for Naomi's sake and for her two grandsons, considering Sister would be their Great Grandma, I have to find out."

"Oh, Aiesha, you are so special! Always wanting to help people. You're going to make a great psychologist someday. I just know it!"

"Thanks to you Momma."

"All of these synchronicities because your empathy and intuition brought you to help Naomi when she got off a bus right outside here lost and distraught. And you went to her rescue."

"Actually it was Davon who...."

Aiesha started to cry again. Pent up tears seemed to become raging rivers flowing out of her eyes. Her Momma hugged her and then sobbed with her. A phrase "the tears of things" popped out of her memory from a book she read once.

This was the first time she had broken down about Davon's death in her Momma's presence. At his funeral and internment, she had stood by his casket stoically dry eyed obviously still in shock about what happened to her boyfriend she had been going out with since junior high. Maya knew how Tyrell envied Davon for being the one Aiesha had chosen to go with. He remained a good friend with Aiesha but always on the sidelines... until, of course, that fateful day when....

Maya and Aiesha blew their noses at the same time then Maya said, "For the love of all Mothers and daughters and especially for the love you and I have for each other, I'm going to help you, Honey. Now what do you want me to do?"

"My plan is to wait a few days, Momma, and then sign up for one of the luncheon cruises after we know Naomi is back at work."

"How are we going to be sure about that?"

"Well, we can call her apartment when her grandsons are most likely at school. If she doesn't answer, we'll presume she's at work."

"But what if she doesn't want to talk to us?"

"I'm banking on the possibility she'll recognize you from the times when she came to the bar to take her daughter home."

"If she does, then I'm sure she's still very angry with me for continuing to serve her beer when she expressly asked me not to. Oh and what about Sister Eustacia?"

"I was hoping maybe after we talk to Naomi, we'll get her to agree to go and visit Sister to find out the truth."

"How are you going to get her to do that?"

"I really don't know yet, Momma. We'll come up with something."

Before Aiesha went to sleep that night, she wrote another

entry in her Journal. "I have the best Momma in the world! She understands me and my intuition. She gets how I accept the truth of synchronicity. She's agreed to help me find out if Sister Eustacia is actually Naomi's Mother and if her daughter Lily is the one my own Momma feels so guilty about. But how could she have known she'd hit her head and bleed to death? She doesn't deserve to keep on carrying around all this guilt! I have to help her clear her conscience."

That night both she and Maya had essentially the same dream....

They were standing together outside the bar, both of them with a big "G" on the front of their shirts. Aiesha looked at her Mother and asked her why, but she simply shook her head and her body but the "G" wouldn't come off. Aiesha tried to pull it off her shirt and then off her Mother's but it growled and bit her hand like a rabid dog.

When the two shared their dreams in the morning, they were astounded at the similarity between them. The only difference was that in Aiesha's dream, she was able to pull off the "G." Maya could not. The significance of this fact didn't escape either of them.

The next Wednesday the two sat down together at one of the long tables on the boat after one of Naomi's grandsons told them she was back on the job. They spotted her at the same time as she came over to ask them for their drink orders. Maya spoke first, "Hello, Naomi. My name is Maya and this is my daughter Aiesha. You talked to her on the phone last week."

"Oh yes, Aiesha. I just couldn't keep talking when you called because I was having an unpleasant reaction to my medications."

"Oh, don't even worry about that, Naomi. I hope you're feeling better today."

What Naomi didn't admit to the young girl was the real reason she couldn't keep talking to her on the phone that day. Anyone who even mentioned her Lovely Lily, her Flower to her sent her whole being reeling. How could this young girl have known her dear daughter? It was a mystery to her, one she had to solve no matter what pain it caused her. Somehow she "knew" she was on the razor's edge of finding out something very important. Her insides churned. Her skin felt prickly. In a corner of herself, she even glowed with girlish anticipation.

"So, Naomi, we would like to talk to you after your shift is over. Will that be all right?"

"Well..." the waitress said, creating a moment of silence.

"Do you remember me, Naomi, from all those years ago?" Maya then bravely inquired.

Before she answered, Aiesha noticed how her eyes changed from blue-green to brown in the blink of an eye. Naomi only responded with a curt "Of course!" as she shuffled off to the next table to ask for those passengers' drink orders.

"Momma, what do you think Naomi meant by 'of course'? 'Of course' she'd meet with us when she's off work or 'of course' she remembered you?"

"I don't know, Honey. I'm sure she must still have some very bad feelings against me. After all, as I've already told you, I probably served the last beer before her daughter...."

"But, Momma, you couldn't have known what...."

"I couldn't have, but that doesn't make me feel any better, Aiesha. Naomi begged me not to serve her, but I let Lily badger me into just one more drink. Oh, I still feel so terrible about letting myself give in to her that last night of her young life!"

The loving Mother and ambitious daughter continued to discuss the various interconnected dramas and traumas for a while. Naomi eventually brought them their beverages and later their lukewarm lunches but seemed to be lost in thought, not acknowledging their earlier conversation in the slightest.

After the plates were cleared and the boat was back in the dock, Maya and Aiesha stood up and looked around for Naomi. Ten minutes passed. She was still nowhere to be seen. Maybe she was furious at Maya or too medicated to deal with all of this. Aiesha was about to find the Captain and ask about Naomi when she turned up at their table and announced, "Whew! Finished at last."

"So where would you like to go to talk, Naomi?"

"There's a coffee shop across the street. I need some caffeine in a hurry to get through the rest of this day." Again instinctively she "knew" she had to be really ready for whatever Maya and her daughter were about to tell her.

Aiesha smiled at Maya as the three of them left the boat. At the café she was the first to speak, "I'm sorry about the other day when I called you, Naomi. I didn't realize your medications were causing you problems. Your grandson was worried about you."

"Well they are worried but my grandsons don't know everything. In fact, I never told them the whole story about all the unacceptable decisions their Mother made over men and booze and drugs and her life in general. Especially how she died. They've suspected a lot over the years, and maybe now have figured out some of it. I just don't want to talk to them about my Lovely Lily, my Flower so when you asked me about her, all I could also think about was my Alan, her Father. It was such a difficult situation. You see, somehow through the hands of fate, I became an orphan. I ended up at a number of foster homes after leaving the Orphanage at a young age. Every family that took me in was quite sickening. Then when I was around twelve, I was adopted by a couple only so they could curry favor with their minister. They found every reason in the book to physically and emotionally abuse me.

Years later I fell for their son who was a few years

younger than me. But when his hateful parents found out I was pregnant with his child, they threw me out because they believed I seduced their only son so he would marry me. The truth was that our doomed love grew out of solacing each other in our unfortunate situations. He despised that his Mother and Father treated me so atrociously, beating me for senseless reasons and yelling at me no matter how hard I tried to please them. To make everything worse, I never got to see Alan again because when they found out I was pregnant with his child, his Father told me he had enlisted in the Army and was sent to the Korean War. Some time later I was told Alan was killed on the other side of the world in that horrid conflict. Then recently I learned it was all a lie to keep me away from him."

"Oh how hideous!" Aiesha gasped.

"I left their house before they had the satisfaction of kicking me out. I would have had to live on the streets, but a really marvelous nun named Sister Eustacia took me in at a mission where I worked doing all kinds of chores and charitable deeds. Months later I gave birth to my Lovely Lily, my Flower. She was so beautiful when she was a baby, free from alcohol and other sins."

"She was beautiful even when I knew her." Maya added.

Everyone sipped their coffee or tea for a solemn moment before Aiesha asked, "Naomi, did I hear you right that a nun named Sister Eustacia helped you?"

"Yes...."

"Well, didn't that old nun who was celebrating her birthday on the luncheon cruise several weeks ago have that same strange name?"

"Yeah, I think I heard someone call her that, Aiesha."

"Could she possibly be the same person?"

"I've wondered about that too. In fact, I tried to find out so I went to see her at Saint Clara's Retirement Home. It ended with only more questions."

"Wow, that's really weird. I just started volunteering there and was assigned to her of all people!"

"So did you learn anything from her?" Naomi asked.

"As you know, she is mostly out of touch with reality. She asked if I knew someone named James she apparently loved a long time ago. Also she rambled on about her angry Father, someone named Mary and all kinds of odd things. But this is the strangest thing Naomi..." Aiesha looked directly into the old Grandmother's eyes. "She mentioned a daughter she lost."

From somewhere in the city, a church bell struck three o'clock. Waiting until after the vibrations ceased, Naomi then answered, "She called herself Mary at some point but my best guess concerning James is that he was a special guy she cared about before she entered the convent." However, she had no answer about the supposed daughter the old nun lost. She only could think about how she lost her own daughter.

"Naomi, were you able to find out anything else?" Maya asked next.

"I tried to determine if she was the same Sister Eustacia who saved my Lovely Lily, my Flower and me when I was down and out, but she kept obsessing about a man named James and then the fact that her Father was extremely strict and didn't like him and then about losing her baby. A daughter."

"But, Naomi, what's your sense about all of this after talking to her? Could she actually be the same nun who helped you and your daughter so long ago?"

"I want to believe that but I can't be sure."

Aiesha was ready now to go out on a limb and ask her the major question of the day and possibly of her life, "Naomi, you know how your eyes turn from blue-green to brown?'

"Yeah, of course. My Lovely Lily, my Flower's did that too."

"Well, I have to tell you this, Sister Eustacia kept going on and on about eyes. When she wasn't enveloped in tears, I noticed her eyes sometimes changed the same way yours do. But they only changed to brown when she was talking about something very dramatic or frightening to her. When something then excited her and made her happy, they changed back to blue-green from brown. That's what makes me suspect there's some connection between you and her."

"Wait a minute," Maya interrupted, "is there any way she

could be your...."

"No, please, that is ridiculous!" Naomi was starting to shake.

"Well, maybe you are the daughter she lost. Maybe they lied when they told her the baby died...." Aiesha stammered.

"Who is 'They?' Seriously, this is just..." Naomi was now noticeably sweating.

"Oh, I don't know but imagine this, what if she met this James before she was a nun and they...."

"Now come on, Honey, your imagination's working overtime now!" Maya felt compelled to interject.

"No, Momma, I think it's a strong possibility." Their eyes met and Maya suddenly felt a rush of energy as she fully decided to champion her daughter's mission.

Now it was Naomi's turn to really put in her two cents' worth. "Listen to me, Aiesha. Yes, I suppose there's some kind of odd outside chance she might be who you say. Yes, I've thought about our eyes changing colors, too, but I can't imagine... I just can't think that...."

Maya now chimed in, "Naomi, remember the first time you came to the bar and found Lily totally soused? You couldn't fathom that your Lovely Lily could ever be so wasted. And now you can't fathom that this confused old nun whose mind is sitting on the boundary of lucidity could possibly have done some things with or maybe without her consent many years ago." Maya was trying to tell Naomi everything Aiesha was suggesting. The good daughter let her Mother continue, knowing they were now on the same page.

"What if Sister was called Mary before she became a nun? What if this James she talks about was a real guy she knew a long time ago before she entered the convent? And, most of all, what if she had his child and it was you, but she was forced by someone like her strict Father to give you away or maybe even told that you went to Heaven so to speak?"

Naomi stared at the woman. She had asked her out loud all the questions she'd unconsciously been asking herself for days. If any of this was true, especially the possibility, remote though it might be, that Sister Eustacia was her Birth Mother she thought was dead, what would she do if she found her now? The Mother who for some reason would have given her away. How could she face her? Most likely the old nun wouldn't be able to verify anything or even understand anything for that matter. She remembered how she kept talking about how she wasn't allowed to say anything to anyone about some secret.

Maya turned away from her stare. She still felt somewhat guilty about her part in how Naomi's daughter died. She had tried to stop her drinking. She had tried to honor her promise to her Mother but... She probably still hadn't forgiven her for what had happened either.

Naomi realized that her friend did still feel guilty about

what happened to her Lovely Lily, her Flower. Then she remembered how she verbally attacked that stranger on the bus unjustly accusing her of killing her daughter. As a result of that mistaken identity she had let go of her anger toward Maya and put it all back on herself where it really belonged. Naomi felt so remorseful for what she did and/or didn't do to change the course of her daughter's short life.

Aiesha wondered what was going through the two other women's heads. She knew her Momma still felt to blame for Lily's demise and Naomi probably still harbored some lingering feelings of loathing toward her. She wondered if she'd ever find out the rest of the story that connected their three lives.

"So, Naomi, what do you think about the possibility that Sister is your Mother?" Aiesha couldn't help but ask.

"I don't know, Aiesha, I'm so taken aback and yet curious. Up one minute and down the next."

"Momma, what do you think? Could all or any of this be true somehow?"

"I thought I knew, but I guess I don't know either, Aiesha. The whole thing about their eyes changing colors is an odd connection. I just don't know what to think."

"Well, I do know one thing, Maya and Aiesha, I have to go back and talk to Sister Eustacia again as soon as I possibly can. She is the only person who can solve this mystery. The trouble is her shaky mind though. The Alzheimer's. It's so hard keeping her in the present and getting her to answer questions directly. So frustrating!"

"I tried to ask her questions the other day when I was there, but she just kept talking about dancing the Charleston and bobbing her hair and loving James, but she wouldn't or couldn't say who he was to her. In fact, she got almost hysterical when I tried to help her take her shoes off to get into bed. I didn't understand what was going on in her head at all." Naomi had stopped shaking and was sitting up straight now, fully focused and attentive.

"Naomi, from what Aiesha read on the Internet about that disease as well as what I've studied, a person with Alzheimer's can flow in and out of the real world remembering minute details from many years ago while at the same time maybe not even knowing the current date. It's really hard to deal with. In the course of a few minutes, my aunt who was recently diagnosed with this condition kept telling her sister, my Mother, at least five times to look at her new hat on the dresser."

All three of them sat there for a second, just absorbing all of the input and emotions.

"I'll tell you what, Naomi and Aiesha," Maya added. "I think the best thing to do now is for the two of you to go and try to talk to the old nun again. Maybe you'll have more success together."

Maya and Aiesha then said good bye to Naomi who

agreed to visit Sister at the home with Aiesha the next week. Naomi had just enough time to connect with Smithy, her ride home.

For at least the third time in the same week, Aiesha scribbled down some quick thoughts in her journal when she got home. "My intuition tells me loud and clear that Sister Eustacia is really Naomi's Mother as hard as that is for anyone to imagine or believe. I know my intuition is pretty good. So what if they are Mother and Daughter though if Sister Eustacia won't even be able to comprehend this. But won't Naomi be glad she finally knows her Mother and at least her Father's first name, if nothing else? Oh, I hope everything works out for both of them.

I've been so lucky to have my Momma in my life. People like Sister and that waitress have lived lives that are so sad. I'm going to try to help as many women like them when I become a psychologist or a psychiatrist or maybe a social worker like Naomi's two grandsons. Also, I've been wondering about what's going to happen with me and Tyrell. Will we become more than just friends like I think he wants us to be? Maybe. For now, though, I can't quite imagine that happening, but he's been so nice to me since Davon's. Oh, I miss him so much! I wonder if he'd mind if Tyrell kind of took his place now. Not that he really could, of course. No one can. Still Tyrell's been my/our bud from like forever. Maybe I should cut him some slack. Maybe I should... Oh I just don't know what to do. I'm so confused."

That night Aiesha had a dream that seemed to allay her concerns about becoming more than just Tyrell's friend....

She was walking to school when a car load of monster looking jocks yelled at her, "Hey hey hey, Isha! Still missing your Davon, huh? Boo Hoo for you, Sweets! How 'bout jumping in this here car with us? We know how to show a pretty little girl like you a fine time!" Aiesha ignored them and kept walking. Then Tyrell with what looked like angel wings sticking out of his shoulder blades appeared and repelled the guys in the car warning them, "No way you'll ever get her! Now get very lost or you will be very sorry!" Then he took Aiesha's hand in his and kissed it just as she woke up.

She knew she had to talk to Tyrell as soon as she could track him down, but first, she called her friend Simone who was in her Psych class to find out her take on the dream.

"Hi, Simone. Do you have a few minutes? I need your perspective. It's serious."

Without wasting any time, Aiesha shared her dream. In her heart of hearts, she knew what it was telling her, but she wanted to hear what her friend thought about it before she did anything concrete to honor it.

"Well, Isha, here's what I think. Hands down it's telling you to call that angel man!"

"What? Simone, Tyrell isn't an angel and second.... oh, I

don't know, I'm so uncertain about this, that's all."

"All I have to say then is what you already know. When the time is right, you'll do what you know you have to do, Aiesha. What your unconscious was telling you up front and personal. Oh, I'm getting another call now from my man Damian. Let's talk again tomorrow, OK?"

Simone hung up then, leaving Aiesha still torn between staying true to Davon's memory and giving Tyrell a chance but, of course, not to take his place. She knew he never could do that, but he could fill the empty place she had in her heart ever since Davon's untimely death.

She decided to get her Momma's opinion on what she should do about Tyrell. As soon as she came home from the bar, she waited until she sat down with a cup of her favorite lemon tea and a blackberry scone. Without any small talk, she asked, "Oh, Momma, what am I going to do about Tyrell? I'm really upset about.... it's just that... oh, I don't know... I...."

"...don't know whether to let him be your new special friend now, right?"

"That's exactly where I am. A real issue."

"So what's your heart say, Honey?"

"It's confused and conflicted and...."

"So do you want your Momma's advice?"

"Of course, you know I always do."

"Before I met your Father, I had a few good guy friends.

Only one of them I thought I might marry some day, but before I knew it, that relationship went down the drain. In the end it was all for the best because I wouldn't have met your Father otherwise."

"But, Momma, at least that other guy didn't die, did he?"

"No, Honey, but for me he did by simply disappearing from my life. I climbed the walls of my apartment for months crying my eyes out every other minute, but finally I realized we simply weren't meant to be together so I had no other choice but to move on. Just think, you wouldn't be here if I hadn't."

"I hear you, Momma, but is it the same thing with Davon and Tyrell and me?"

"No one can tell you that, Aiesha. Only you know in your heart of hearts. Listen to it. And now I have to get to bed. Good night, Honey. Remember that French expression I taught you when you were little, 'Faites les beaux reves.'"

"Night, Momma. I hope I will have some good dreams too. Thanks for your thoughts. I love you."

"And you know how much I love you and I think Tyrell does as well."

When her Momma left the room after overwhelming her with what seemed like an afterthought that Aiesha knew was purposeful, she sat staring out the picture window in the living room into the starry night wondering what Davon would tell her to do now. She closed her eyes.

Out of the dark of the sky, she saw him float into the room. When she felt him hold her hand, she shivered and "heard" him say, "Listen to your Momma. She knows."

Jerked awake by this awareness, Aiesha rubbed her eyes looking around the room for any sign of her lost friend. Already startled, she almost fell off the sofa when her cell phone pierced the serene night air. And she almost dropped the phone when she saw Tyrell's number on the display.

"Hi, Isha, how you doing tonight?"

"Oh, my Momma and I were just talking about you."

"Really. What about? My smile? My smarts? My body?"

"You're so full of yourself, Tyrell! But I like you anyway."

"Well, thanks for that. Let's get together soon, OK? I need to hear more about this conversation between you and your Momma."

"Sure. Call me tomorrow and I'll see when I can fit you into my busy schedule."

"We're on. Sleep well. I...."

As fate would have it, Aiesha closed her phone before she heard the rest of Tyrell's statement. Instinctively she knew that he had always loved her if that was even what he was going to say. How understanding and sympathetic he'd been to her since Davon was killed. He'd watched over her almost better than a guardian angel. They would have to have a serious conversation soon. Very soon. First she had to decide what she actually felt or could feel for him. The words she "heard" from Davon, "Listen to your Momma. She knows," seemed to refer directly to the fact that Tyrell really cared for her or maybe even loved her. Now what was she going to do about that?

The next day Aiesha agreed to go to Francie's with Tyrell. As they enjoyed their strawberry sundaes, Aiesha smiled as she admitted to him, "I haven't been very nice to you, have I, since...."

Afraid she was going to break down, Tyrell quickly jumped in, "No, Isha, but I understand. It's been a hard time for you, but I have to admit for me too."

"Oh, Tyrell, I keep thinking if only I hadn't put off Davon until later that night, he would be...."

"But how do you know that for sure, Isha? Anything else could have happened. It was in no way your fault! Believe that once and forever!"

"I feel bad too that I haven't been thinking about you and how you must be missing your best guy friend from whenever, right?"

"Yeah, I've been feeling down like you, but I know Davon wouldn't want us to be hanging round all sad. He'd want us to get on with our lives. So let's think about the future and not the past we can't do anything about, OK?"

"You're a wise man, Tyrell. Thanks for putting all of our

pain in some kind of perspective."

"So are we good say for a second date next Saturday?"

"Sure. Come over around 8. I'll be ready."

Tyrell dropped his long-time friend off at her house and kissed her on the cheek at the door. Aiesha smiled and waved good bye to him as he pulled his Mustang away from the curb. She was glad her Momma was still up when she walked in the living room. She had so much more to talk to her about.

"So did you and Tyrell have a good time, Honey?"

"Oh, Momma, it was almost like the old days except without Davon. We both miss him so much. We're going out again next weekend."

"I'm so happy for the both of you, Aiesha."

"You know what, Momma, I think Tyrell and I are on the right track. We plan to take it slow, but maybe there's a future out there for the two of us. In the meantime I have a really big question that has been bothering me a lot since we talked about that girl Lily and how bad you still feel about your part in what happened to her. How have you been dealing with that guilt all this time?"

"It hasn't been easy, Honey, I'll tell you that. I talk to myself a lot trying to convince my conscience that circumstances went way beyond my control. Lily made choices I couldn't change... I got nowhere trying to control her. Yet it was only when I finally talked it all out to her Mother and shared all the depressing feelings I had that I started to kick the guilt out of my heart. Not that it's all gone away yet. I guess that it'll never be, but at least I can live with it easier now."

"Oh, I hope that works for me too, Momma. I feel so bad that Davon was coming over to see me later the night when he was killed. If only I had let him stay earlier...."

"Don't do that to yourself, Honey. What's done is done. You have to let yourself get on with your life. That's what Davon would want for you. I'm sure Tyrell will stay around to help you. Come on now, let's both get a good night's sleep."

Aiesha and her Mother hugged each other as they walked upstairs together. Aiesha decided to write a journal entry before she went to sleep.

"Believe it or not, Tyrell and I are going to go out again next weekend. I feel OK about this and so does Tyrell. Actually, we both feel Davon would be fine with this too. I talk to him in my head sometimes telling him what's happening with Tyrell and also with Naomi and Sister Eustacia and all the synchronistic connections going on. All the odd stuff like their chameleon-like eyes. I reminded him he met Naomi when he gave her the ride of her life on his bike to get her to her job on the cruise boat. But then there is Sister, whose mind is out of whack probably from Alzheimer's. I think she is Naomi's Mother who she thought was dead. I'll tell you what, though, facing your passing and then meeting Sister Eustacia has taught me to appreciate life while I have it. Since it is so very precious, I have to live it one day or one minute at a time, not regretting the past, enjoying the present and hopeful for the future."

Noticing the time, she then continued, "I have to say Good Night now, Davon. I'll never forget you."

Chapter 9

Questions Answered?

The next Thursday Aiesha and Naomi met each other in the lobby of Saint Clara's and walked together to Sister Eustacia's room. It was the first day of Spring and the hallway was full of flowery decorations and Easter-themed posters. When they walked into her sun-filled room, they noticed the old nun had apparently pulled off her headpiece and tossed it across the room.

As she sat in her wheel chair, she kept pulling at the ends of her cropped hair which was longer than it would have been many years before if it had been bobbed as she had previously intimated. However, now she kept yanking at it mumbling, "Grow! Get longer. Father doesn't like it bobbed. He's so angry at me but especially at poor James for letting me do this."

For a few minutes Sister didn't realize that anyone had

come into her room. She kept pulling at her hair and then started chanting, "James. Eyes so blue-green. Oh, James! Oh, James, where are you? What has become of you?"

She became very quiet abruptly when she noticed the two women standing beside her.

"Hello, Sister. It's me Aiesha. Look who's here with me. Naomi."

"Aiesha? Hello, Honey. And who's this Naomi woman you brought with you?"

"Don't you remember me, Sister? We talked a few weeks ago. I was your waitress on your birthday cruise."

"The one on the Ile de France on my sixteenth birthday?"

"Well, no."

"Do you have news about where James is then?'

"Who is James, Sister? We really want to know."

"My One and Onl... Oh no, I can't say that! Father told me I can't talk about him."

"But isn't your Father dead now, Sister?"

"Well, yes, I suppose, he jumped out of a window. But no, not if I just celebrated my sixteenth birthday party and ate my cake too on the Ile de France on the way to Paris. No! No! Father will be so angry if he finds out what happened because of what James and I did."

"What did you and James do, Sister?"

"In bed we... No! Tell me you didn't hear me say that...

My name's Mary. It's my sixteenth birthday... we're celebrating on the Ile de France going to Paris... James is in my stateroom... No, I'm in his. Now Father's pulling me out of there!.. Oh, I'm so confused and scared! I don't know what he's going to do to us!"

Then Sister started to cry, huge waterfalls gushing down the ridges of her weathered face. Naomi handed her some tissues and asked, "Sister, was your name Mary before...."

"Yes, that's who I am, Mary, Mary quite contrary. And James came into my garden."

Sister giggled then like a young girl and Aiesha and Naomi looked at each other wondering if they were both thinking the same thing. Could this old nun actually be referring to having relations with a man named James when she was still a girl named Mary? She would have had to be only about as old as Aiesha then. Maybe even younger.

Before they could ask each other, Sister started chanting again, "Eyes blue-green. Eyes blue-green. Oh how I love you! Oh, how I love you! My James. My James." In hindsight, it was as if her ramblings about James' eyes were an unwitting clue to anyone who would listen and care enough to figure out the truth.

She then stopped ranting for some reason as her face lit up with what appeared to be an overwhelming awareness. "James came to see me. He was old like me and I didn't realize...." she fumbled for words as her eyes went from blue-green to brown.

With tears flowing down her aged face, she remembered

what he told her that day word for word...

"Oh my dear dear Mary, how I longed to see you over all these years. I gave the Orphanage where our daughter was sent the money your Father bribed me with. For the last fifty years I've been a monk in a contemplative order in California doing penance for taking away your innocence. Oh, please forgive me, dearest Mary."

Sister Eustacia could see into his sad eyes as he was spilling his soul to her. As she relived these moments, she watched his eyes change from blue-green to brown. James' eyes could change just like her own.

As these memories flitted through her oft bemused mind, she looked directly into Naomi's blue-green eyes and with an instant flash of insight, the seventy-eight year old previously motherless woman, finally knew this was her real Birth Mother! What an incredible feeling swept through her whole body. On this first day of Spring, she felt reborn, like she had been granted a new life. She discerned at the same time that this ninety-five year old woman may never be able to comprehend that fact, so instead of sharing her insight with Sister Eustacia she smiled at her and kissed her hands.

To her astonishment, Sister purred in response, "Oh James, you are such a gentleman! No, I don't think I can stay in your room tonight though. Oh James, you're tickling me so. Oh James! Oh James! Oh!"

Naomi slipped her hand away from the nun's. It felt so awfully strange that her Mother was thinking she was her Father!

Aiesha watched only vaguely imagining the inner drama evolving in front of her. She couldn't wait to ask Naomi what had just happened. Still she was as sure as sunset that it was something major. Something monumental. Something life changing, certainly for Naomi.

All of a sudden both Aiesha and Naomi were taken off guard when Sister creaked up from her wheelchair, looked directly at Naomi and announced, "No, our baby was not born dead. She's right here!"

At that she grabbed Aiesha's hand, pulled her into her shaking arms and hugged her tightly! Naomi could only watch dumbfounded yet somehow understanding. None of the questions mattered anymore because now she knew she had a Mother. For some reason she couldn't fathom, it was of no concern that she was too disoriented to understand this significant fact.

The only vital aspect was that Naomi finally found her long lost Mother, a true Lady Baltimore, who had lived most of her life in a cloud of unknowing about her daughter and James. As a nun, she continued to do penance for her actions at sixteen before she hardly knew a thing about the world and its men.

Naomi smiled as she watched Aiesha standing in the old nun's embrace holding her hand and feeling alternately embarrassed and elated for reasons she couldn't express. She noticed then that her Mother's eyes were no longer bloodshot and changed from brown to a sparkling blue-green.

Several minutes later when the nurse came in the room, she was overwhelmed to see Sister Eustacia hugging a wrinkled white woman and a young black girl.

She remarked in astonishment to Naomi, who was finally at peace and smiling widely, "Life is so strange. As I live and breathe, I'll never comprehend the beauty of it!"

Epilogue

A week after their strange reunion, Naomi was sitting by her Mother's bedside when she heard her mumble and then call out with an increasingly loud voice, "James. Your eyes so blue. So green. Oh James!" She tossed and turned in her bed throughout the afternoon and then just as the sun went down, she grabbed Naomi's hand and moaned softly, "Oh my baby!" then breathed her last. She would never know for sure, but Naomi believed that in a burst of lucidity at the last moment of Sister's life, she realized that Naomi was actually her daughter who was taken from her. She would always be grateful for that gift. She held her still warm gnarled hand for a long time before calling the nurse.

With her grandsons, her new Lily, and Aiesha and her Mother, Naomi attended Sister's funeral at Saint Clara's Retirement Home all of them vowing to stay in touch to honor the woman who unwittingly had brought them all together.

Naomi became a surrogate Grandmother to Aiesha; her grandsons became Aiesha's good friends. Maya and Naomi frequently met for lunch and talked a lot about Lily and Fate. Each time they both felt somewhat better about their respective guilt in the inexorable events leading up to the young woman's tragic departure from this world.

Two years later Tom and Ted served as Best Men and Simone as Maid of Honor for Aiesha and Tyrell's May wedding on the same ship in the Baltimore Harbor where Naomi used to work. Aiesha's best friends from high school were the bridesmaids while Tyrell's four brothers were their escorts. Aiesha's little sister was the ring bearer. Naomi stood holding Maya's hand throughout the ceremony. A bond had continued to grow between them.

All of the families including their newly found Aunt Lily attended Tom and Ted's graduation from graduate school the following fall. When the two brothers began working at a shelter in the area, the newlyweds volunteered to help them out on Saturdays and during the week when they were free after their college classes, Aiesha's in psychology and Tyrell's in criminal justice.

Every month Naomi visits Sister Eustacia's grave site on the grounds of Saint Clara's Retirement Home to thank her for being a true Lady Baltimore but, most of all, for being the Mother she sadly never knew until the end of her life.

She was also grateful to know that the man named James her Mother always talked about was most likely her Father. She felt so blessed finally knowing about both of them, but especially thankful for them giving her the life she now cherishes every day.

For now she lives it to the hilt and loves it, with Jesus' words from the Last Supper in St. John's Gospel giving her continued solace, "I will see you again and your heart shall rejoice and your joy no man shall take from you."

THE END

Lifetime Television Welcomed Author Rose Gordy to Hit TV Show The Balancing Act

On June 24th 2011 Lifetime TV interviewed Rose Gordy about her dramatic life and her book "Unsettled Lives"

PRLog (Press Release) (Pompano Beach, FL) After the economy crashed in 2008, many people lost their homes and nest eggs, but worst of all they were left with unsettled lives and uncertainty. With the economic crisis ongoing, people are searching for solace, resolution and a new acceptable normal. On June 24th, 2011, The Balancing Act TV show on Lifetime interviewed Rose Gordy about how she has weathered the storm and her new book "Unsettled Lives."

Author and dream counselor Rose Gordy spent thirteen years of her early life as a nun effectively cut off from the "the world of the flesh and the devil." Through her experiences in the convent as well as decades of teaching in the classroom, she has woven a compelling story honoring the lives lost and changed forever by triumph and adversity.

"Unsettled Lives - A Collection of Short Stories" presents numerous tales of people caught in the second-guessing, soul-searching, and uncertain decision-making periods of their lives. In dealing with their lives of quiet and not so quiet desperation, the book's characters may rise above the pain and face new tomorrows with hope and joy. Or perhaps some of them may find their fate in hapless distress and melancholy. What threads of life's twists and turns will determine the direction and destiny that awaits them?

"Having Rose Gordy on 'The Balancing Act' has brought yet another inspiring story of perseverance to women, one that will have a real impact, and help them balance their lives. This is the essence of solutions-based programming, and we're proud that we can bring this to a wide audience."

To view the interview, please visit www.Rosewords.com.

Rose's stories, poems and essays have appeared in the following publications, among others:

Association for the Study of Dreams Newsletter
Burning Light
Dream Network Journal
Futuremics
Ginseng
Ideas Plus of The English Journal
Jungian Literary Criticism
Mad Alley
Networker of the Women Business Owners
  of Montgomery County, Maryland
New Women - New Church
Pablo Lennis
Pittsburgh Mercy
The Critic
The Dana California Literary Society
The Journal of the National Association of Poetry Therapy
The Journal of the National Council of Teachers of English
The Maryland English Journal
The Merton Seasonal

"Into the Green Unknown" and Other Science Fiction Stories - Now Available in Paperback

Attention Earth People...Special Announcement about an Interstellar Book by Rose of Maryland

PRLog (Press Release) – Heralding the release of Rose Gordy's book, "Into the Green Unknown," a collection of 21 science fiction stories and 6 poems, available now at Rosewords.com.

Years in the making, these astounding adventures range from everyday events turned bizarre, to fantastic realms under Earth's oceans, to incredible worlds beyond human perception. Stories such as "The Announcement," "Living Waters At Lucia," and "The Man From Somewhere Else" take readers to strange places they can't possibly journey. Or can they...?

In "Subterfuge," will Madame President be able to protect L.A. from take over by mind-controlling visitors? In "Lost Tides," can two nervous parents protect their children from a celestial disaster and its ramifications? In "The Genetic Casino," will the abducted Ronatta want to discover how she was chosen or remain ignorant and blissful? At the frenetic pace modern science is progressing these tales may be science fact by the time you cast an eye over them. That is, if they have not already transpired....

So join us for a jaunt on the Earth, in the Earth, in the Clouds, and among the Stars.

"Into the Green Unknown" is available now in paperback for only $14.99 and can be ordered at http://www.Rosewords.com. At Rosewords.com you can learn more about Rose Gordy's books and other projects. Bon Voyage!

ISBN: 1456528904

"Stairs to the Attic - A Collection of Poems" - Available Now in Paperback & Kindle eBook

A sweeping compilation of poems by Rose Gordy illustrating an unusual earthly life relevant to society's oxymorons.

PRLog (Press Release) – Rosewords Books is pleased to announce a new book by Rose Gordy. Titled "Stairs to the Attic - A Collection of Poems," this tome is now available for purchase on the Rosewords Books website, www.Rosewords.com. This is the fourth book by Rose of Maryland, following "Into The Green Unknown," "The Ladies Baltimore," and "Unsettled Lives."

"Stairs to the Attic," a book which instinctually eschews the conventional, presents a collection of poetry down to earth yet otherworldy. Amidst the hundreds of little adventures within these pages, readers will no doubt find themselves transported to places and feelings familiar and fantastic. One could watch TV but nothing captures an experience like the timeless rhythmical synergy of song & speech which Humans call Poetry.

The poem which gives this book its title, Stairs to the Attic, paints a picture of youth restrained but always one step away from the truth. Will a group of ex-nuns find out the secret their convent held from them? What could possibly happen when these liberated women return decades later full of latent curiosity?

Other poems delve into the dreamscape, the synchronistic, the blood bonds, the shadow memories, the earthiness, the maternal instincts, the harkening forward and the eyeful. Filled with 38original photographs and over 140 poems this unusual book will break the proverbial mold.

"Stairs to the Attic" is available in paperback for $14.99 and can be ordered through the publisher's website: Rosewords.com.
ISBN: 1466226269

Author Rose Gordy's e-books are now available on Apple's iBookstore and Amazon's Kindle

Rosewords Books has released Rose's published tomes for the iPad, iPhone, and Kindle e-Readers

PRLog (Press Release) – Rosewords Books is pleased to announce the publication of Rose Gordy's four books in electronic book format. With e-book sales now surpassing print book sales on Amazon, the state of the book business is transitioning to a new and exciting era. Accordingly, Rosewords Books now has e-books for sale on Apple's iBookstore, where over 100 million e-books have been sold, and Amazon's Kindle Store, the industry leader in e-book sales.

Before the advent of electronic books, author and dream counselor Rose Gordy spent thirteen years of her early life as a nun effectively cut off from the world. In spite of the conditions within the church, she managed to leave and make a life for herself including getting married and having three sons. Through her experiences in the convent as well as decades of teaching in the classroom, she has written books which honor the lives lost and changed forever by triumph and adversity.

Her four books are titled "Stairs to the Attic,""Unsettled Lives," "The Ladies Baltimore: Mothers and Daughters Alone and Together" and "Into the Green Unknown." All are available at Rosewords.com.

"Unsettled Lives" - A Collection of Short Stories - Available Now at Rosewords.com

A wide-ranging collection of short stories delving into the unstrung lives and rattled experiences of modern society.

PRLog (Press Release) – Rosewords Books is pleased to announce a new book by Rose Gordy and a completely redesigned Rosewords website. Rose's latest book is duly titled "Unsettled Lives - A Collection of Short Stories" and is now available for purchase on the state-of-the-art Rosewords Books website, http://www.Rosewords.com. This is the third book by Rose of Maryland, following "Into The Green Unknown" and "The Ladies Baltimore."

"Unsettled Lives - A Collection of Short Stories" presents numerous tales of people caught in the second-guessing, soul-searching, and uncertain decision-making periods of their lives. Will the myriad characters opt for the "right" path seemingly laid out for them? Yes, they may eventually find their way... but all too often they shall otherwise stumble into unexpected and unique journeys we call the "Human Experience."

Throughout 21 short stories, numerous situations of emotional and social consequence will be offered to the reader. In "Lila, The Love of His Lonely Life," will Charles ever come to grips with his ephemeral obsession? What is Sister Alberta in "Masquerades" aiming to discover by ingenious cloak-and-dagger operations? Furthermore, what could the doctor In "Joy's Esperanza" tell open-minded Joy that would send her into serious self-doubt?

So please join us for psychological jaunts into the various lives within "Unsettled Lives" ... and don't forget to choose the right door in your own.

"Unsettled Lives" is available in paperback for $14.99 and can be ordered through http://www.Rosewords.com. ISBN: 1456420097

www.Rosewords.com

44626377R00139

Made in the USA
Middletown, DE
12 June 2017